What's happening to Duncan's brains?

I thought I smelled something burning. I wanted to stop, but it was as if my hand was on automatic pilot, and my brain was too busy getting fried to give it a new order.

Z-A-A-A-P!

That sound, like an enormous spark sizzling through the night was the last thing I remember. I blacked out, and fell to the floor.

Books by Bruce Coville

Camp Haunted Hills:
    How I Survived My Summer Vacation
    Some of My Best Friends Are Monsters
    The Dinosaur That Followed Me Home

Magic Shop Books:
    Jennifer Murdley's Toad
    Jeremy Thatcher, Dragon Hatcher
    The Monster's Ring

My Teacher Books:
    My Teacher Is an Alien
    My Teacher Fried My Brains
    My Teacher Glows in the Dark
    My Teacher Flunked the Planet

Goblins in the Castle

Monster of the Year

Space Brat

Available from MINSTREL® Books

My Teacher Fried My Brains

by
Bruce Coville

Illustrated by
John Pierard

A GLC Book

A MINSTREL® BOOK

PUBLISHED BY POCKET BOOKS

New York   London   Toronto   Sydney   Tokyo   Singapore

To Byron,
because the first one
changed my life—and
because he asked for it.

This book is a work of fiction. Names, characters, places and incidents are
either the product of the author's imagination or are used fictitiously. Any
resemblance to actual events or locales or persons, living or dead, is entirely
coincidental.

A MINSTREL PAPERBACK *ORIGINAL*

 A Minstrel Book published by
POCKET BOOKS, a division of Simon & Schuster
1230 Avenue of the Americas, New York, NY 10020

Copyright © 1991 by General Licensing Company, Inc.
Cover artwork copyright © 1991 by General Licensing Company, Inc.

Special thanks to Pat MacDonald, Tisha Hamilton, and Adam and Cara Coville.

Cover painting by Steven Fastner.
Illustrations by John Pierard
Book Design by Paula Keller
Developed by Byron Preiss and Daniel Weiss

Senior Editor: Sarah Feldman
Assistant Editor: Kathy Huck
All right reserved, including the right to reproduce this book
or portions thereof in any form whatsoever.
For information address Simon & Schuster
1230 Avenue of the Americas, New York, NY 10020

ISBN: 0–671–72710–9

First Minstrel Books Printing June 1991
20 19 18 17 16 15 14 13 12 11 10 9

A MINSTREL BOOK and colophon are registered trademarks of Simon &
Schuster

My Teacher
Fried My Brains

CHAPTER ONE

First Day Blues

I was standing in the bathroom, brushing my teeth, when I looked up and saw a horrible green face in the mirror.

"Hey, Duncan," rasped a voice from behind me, "what time is it?"

A wave of terror washed over me. "Go away!" I yelled, spattering toothpaste foam across the mirror.

"Wrong answer!" shouted the face. "It's not go-away time, it's *bopping* time!"

A strong arm wrapped around my neck. "Help!" I screamed. "Aliens!" But even as I was screaming, I saw in the mirror that the arm holding me was a strong human arm.

"Patrick!" I shouted, mad now instead of terrified. "Come on, Patrick, cut it *ow!*"

I said "OW!" instead of "out" because Patrick had just landed a major noogie on my skull. I would tell you why my big brother was beating on me if I could, but I can't, because I don't know. He just does that sometimes. I do it to other people. You know how it is: you get upset, things build up inside you, and suddenly you BOP! someone.

Or maybe you don't. But that's how things work in our family.

Patrick gave me another noogie.

"You creep!" I screamed, trying to wriggle out of his grip. "Get out of here!"

"Quiet up there!" shouted our father.

I would have yelled for him to make Patrick leave me alone, but it wouldn't do any good. Dad's theory is that life is rough, and I might as well get used to it. That may be true, but I've noticed that when I hit kids in school none of the teachers say, "Why, Duncan, what a good lesson you've just given little Jimmy in the fact that life is rough." What they usually say is, "Look, you little jerk, I've had about enough of your antics. One more stunt like that and you're heading straight to the principal's office!" Or if they're feeling particularly nice they might say, "Now, Duncan, that's not how we solve our problems, is it?"

It is in our family. What planet are these teachers from?

"What planet are they from?"—a good question, considering what had been going on around our town.

See, things had been pretty tense in Kennituck Falls since last spring, when this alien named Broxholm kidnapped weird Peter Thompson and took him off into space. Even though Broxholm was gone, people were still frightened—as if they thought there were aliens still lurking around, waiting to grab people.

With the grown-ups that scared, you can be sure kids around here had about the worst summer ever, mostly because parents were afraid to let their little darlings out of the house. It seemed like the town motto was, "I don't want *you* disappearing like that Peter Thompson." (Well, my parents didn't say that. But most of the others did.) I bet a hundred years from now people in this town will still be telling their kids that if they don't behave an alien boogey man will get them.

To make things worse, Peter Thompson's father—who didn't really give a poop about Peter when he was here—had decided that he really missed his son.

Mr. Thompson had come up to me in the park one day. "You know where he is, don't you?" he said. "You know where they took my boy."

I had stared at him for a moment. Mr. Thompson was skinnier than he used to be, and there were dark circles under his eyes. Then I remembered what Peter had said when he let me stay in his house to hide from the alien: "Don't worry about my father. He won't mind. He won't even know!"

It had been true. Mr. Thompson was almost

never there, and when he was, he didn't pay any attention to Peter at all.

So I had looked at him, all skinny and sad, and said, "What do you care where he is?" Then I ran away because I was afraid he was going to hit me. I suppose it was a pretty rotten thing for me to say, but I had a feeling that the main reason Mr. Thompson was so upset was that everyone else thought he should be.

To tell you the truth, I kind of missed old Peter myself. Everyone used to think I hated him. That wasn't true. I just picked on him because I didn't know what else to do with him.

Well, maybe I did hate him a little, because he was so smart and I was so dumb. Except I wasn't really dumb. I just *thought* I was. Of course, my family and my teachers had given me a lot of help in coming to that conclusion.

I was feeling plenty dumb when I got to school that morning. First of all, I was late because of the fight with Patrick. Second, my head hurt where my father had whacked me afterward. (At least he whacked Pat, too. He always treated us both the same way when it came to that.) Third, I couldn't find my classes, so I kept walking in on things that were already in session.

The reason I couldn't find my classes was that it was the first day of school, and I had never been in the building before.

The reason I had never been in the building

4

was that I had played hookey the day we had our junior high orientation tour. I'd figured there was no point in going, since I hadn't expected to pass the sixth grade. (I think the only reason I did pass, which was kind of a shock, was that after what happened with the alien the school decided to pass our whole class out of sympathy or something.)

Well, the first day in a new school is hard enough if you get there on time and have some idea of what's going on. You don't really need things like walking in late and having some big, tall man with black hair and eyes like coal grab your arm and say, "Not off to a very good start, are we, Mr. Dougal?"

"Aaaahh!" I shouted. "Leave me alone!"

That seemed to startle the man. (Actually, it startled me, too. But the way he grabbed me reminded me of the first time I had met Broxholm, when he was pretending to be a substitute teacher and stopped me from beating up on Peter Thompson.)

"Stop that!" said the man, giving me a shake.

I stopped, mostly because I had recognized him. He was the assistant principal. His name was Manuel Ketchum, and he had come to work at our school last spring, after the old assistant principal had a nervous breakdown. According to my brother Patrick, Mr. Ketchum was a real beast. Most kids called him "the Mancatcher" when he wasn't around.

I guess the Mancatcher must have heard of me, too.

"I've been warned to keep an eye on you, Mr. Dougal," he said. "I can see why already."

He asked me for an excuse for being late, which I didn't have. Then he gave me a lecture about punctuality and responsibility, which made me even later for where I was trying to go.

I had to stick my head into three rooms before I found the one where I belonged. Each time I did, I could hear kids snickering when I left. That really fried me. I *hate* it when people laugh at me.

It was almost as bad when I finally did find the right room. It was home economics class! I couldn't believe they had scheduled me for home economics.

Fortunately the teacher was a real babe. And she smiled when she saw me come in! That was the first nice thing that had happened all day.

"Are you Duncan Dougal?" she asked in a kindly voice. When I nodded she smiled again and said, "My name is Miss Karpou. I'm glad you finally made it."

"She'll change her mind once she gets to know him," someone whispered.

The people who heard it started to laugh. I started to blush. If I could have figured out who said it, I would have whapped the jerk.

I did notice it was kind of nervous laughter. In fact, the whole seventh grade seemed a little twitchy that day. Kids are always a little nervous the first day of school, of course. But this was something more. I think being back in school had everyone thinking about the alien again.

Ms. Karpou went back to what she was talking about, which was how to use the equipment without hurting ourselves. Except she wasn't very good at it, because she managed to burn herself almost immediately.

"Ouch!" she cried. She popped her finger into her mouth, then spun around and bent over the counter. For a minute I was afraid she was going to cry. Instead, she turned and ran out of the room.

I felt bad. Miss Karpou was young, she was pretty, and she had been nice to me. I didn't want her to be sad.

The class got a little rowdy then, and pretty soon the Mancatcher came in to shut us up.

Naturally, he blamed everything on me.

As if things weren't bad enough already, at lunchtime this huge eighth grader named Orville Plumber (which is probably half his problem anyway) came up to my table and said, "Hey, kid—you Duncan Dougal?"

I looked up and said, "What about it?"

Orville smiled, a big, nasty, gap-toothed smile, and said, "I'm gonna turn you into dog meat."

CHAPTER TWO

An Alarming Situation

I've been held back a couple of times, so I'm bigger than most kids in my class. But Orville was like a small mountain. I swallowed hard.

This Vietnamese kid named Phon Le Duc started to giggle. "Go get him, Duncan," he said.

I could have killed Phon for that. The problem was, I nearly *had* killed him a couple of times last year, since I used to beat him up about once a month. So I could see why he would have been happy to watch Orville cream me.

"What did I do?" I asked, stalling for time.

"Nothing," said Orville. "I just don't like your face. Come on outside so I can rearrange it."

"Oh, shut up and sit down," said a voice from behind me.

It was Susan Simmons—the girl who had unmasked the alien last spring.

Susan Simmons, one of the five best-looking girls in seventh grade.

Susan Simmons, who was probably the smartest kid in our class, now that weird Peter Thompson was gone.

Susan Simmons, who walked up to Orville Plumber and said, "Go away." That's all she did—just said, "Go away."

You want to know the amazing thing? Orville went. Actually, the first thing he did was turn pale. *Then* he went.

I turned to Susan. "How did you do that?" I asked.

She shrugged. "Ever since last spring a lot of people have been afraid of me. The dumber they are, the more they're afraid. Orville probably thinks I stole some secret weapon from Broxholm and I was ready to use it to drill a hole through his skull."

"Is that true?" I asked, remembering the way Broxholm had melted the school doors shut when he was making his getaway. I also remembered how much time Susan had spent exploring Broxholm's house. Maybe she *had* found something there.

She just smiled and said, "What do you think, Duncan?"

Then she turned and walked back to her own table.

I was frustrated. I wanted to talk to Susan some more. I felt good when I was with her. But she had her own group of friends, and just because I had helped her fight the alien didn't mean she was going to let me in. OK, I guess I hadn't really helped. But I'd been involved! Me, Susan, and

Peter—we were the only ones who had really known what was going on. You'd think that would count for something.

I was also embarrassed, since it doesn't look good to have a girl save you from being turned into dog meat.

Things didn't get any better after lunch. I still hadn't figured out how to get around the building, so I was really late for my sixth-period class, which was math. I tried hard to find it—I really did. I had promised myself I would do better in school this year. (So far that idea wasn't working out very well.) Also, I knew kids would laugh if I came in late again, especially if they had already heard about Susan saving me from Orville. To top things off, I knew from Patrick that the math teacher, Mr. Black, was pretty cranky.

So I really wanted to get there on time.

I kept running up and down hallways, looking for Mr. Black's room. My brain felt like it was melting. I couldn't make any sense of the building. When I finally did find the room I was panting and my heart was pounding.

"Ah, Mr. Dougal, I presume," said Mr. Black when I walked in. "I will accept your lateness today. However, in the future either be here on time or plan to spend the period in the office."

I had had it. Between my brother, my father, the Mancatcher, and Orville Plumber, I just wasn't ready to have anyone else dump on me—

especially when I had been trying so hard to do something right.

Does your mouth ever do things without getting your permission first? Mine does. It did it right then. I looked at Mr. Black and my mouth said, "Bug off, pinhead!"

About three seconds after the words came out of my mouth I realized what I had done. My skin turned cold. At the same time I felt a hand grab my arm.

"What did you say?" asked Mr. Black, yanking me around and staring into my face.

"Nothing," I whispered. "I didn't say anything."

Mr. Black pulled open the door and shoved me through it. "You can try again tomorrow, Mr. Dougal. For today, I think you'll be better off out here."

Inside I could hear the kids laughing.

I really hate it when people laugh at me.

If Mr. Black thought I was going to stand in the hall until the end of the period, he was wrong. I was getting out: out of his hall, and out of his school.

I was heading down the hall when I saw the fire alarm. I figured since I was leaving, everyone else might as well leave, too.

That's not true. I don't know what I figured. I just know that I reached out and pulled it.

The bell started to clang. Doors flew open.

Screaming kids poured out of the classrooms. "It's the aliens!" they cried. "The aliens are back!"

It should have been funny. It would have been funny, if not for one terrible fact: when I pulled the alarm, it sprayed purple ink all over my hand! It didn't take much brainpower to figure out that the ink was to mark people who turned in false alarms.

I had to wash the stuff off. I ran for the boys' room.

Duh! Brilliant move, Duncan. That's exactly what they expect you to do—which shouldn't have been too hard to figure out, except I was either too scared or too stupid to manage it. Fortunately, my brother had warned me about this.

I shot back into the hallway. Things were still in an uproar. Some kids were actually crying because they were convinced the alien invasion had begun. Teachers were shouting and trying to get them out of the building.

As fire drills go, this was a total disaster.

Jamming my purple hand in my pocket, I pushed through the confusion and headed for the back door of the school. The door opened onto a loading dock. Three or four empty cardboard boxes were stacked at the far end. Closer to me stood a big green dumpster, already starting to stink in the afternoon heat.

What I really wanted to do was take off and

run. But since about half the school was outside already, I couldn't do that without being caught. I had to hide someplace.

Well, at least I wasn't in the boys' room. I figured the Mancatcher was there right now, looking for a kid with a purple hand.

I pulled my hand out of my pocket and stared at the purple stain. It was like a big sign that shrieked, "Duncan did it! *Duncan did it!*"

Where could I hide? I peeked back around the door. Things were quieter now. Maybe I could hide someplace inside until school was over.

I opened the door, slipped through, and almost swallowed my tongue.

The Mancatcher was heading right toward me.

CHAPTER THREE

An Extra Hand

I shot back out the door and looked around in desperation. Where could I go?

I could see only one place where no one would look for me.

The dumpster.

The Mancatcher would be coming through the door soon. No time to think—only to do. I ran across the loading dock, grabbed the lip of the dumpster, and swung my leg over the edge.

When I looked down inside I almost changed my mind. Four feet below me waited a smelly mass of banana peels, bread crusts, half-eaten hamburgers, and things too gross to mention. I considered turning back. Then I heard the door start to swing open.

Taking a deep breath, I swung my other leg over and dropped into the dumpster.

My feet sank several inches into the trash. A cloud of fruit flies swarmed around my head. It was like jumping into a swamp. The only thing I didn't get was the smell. That was because I was holding my breath.

I crouched there in the trash, listening for Mancatcher sounds. After a few seconds I heard him say, "Is somebody out here?"

I let out a sigh of relief. (A soft sigh.) If the Mancatcher had spotted me, he would have been calling my name, not just asking for "someone." So he hadn't seen me—at least, not well enough to know it was me. It was the first break I had had all day.

In a little while I heard the door open and close again. I started to relax. But suddenly I realized he might be trying a trick—making it sound like he had gone, so anyone out here would think it was safe to stop hiding.

I decided I had better stay right where I was. The only move I made was to shift around slightly so I could sit down. As I did, I could feel stuff smearing all over me. Something wet started soaking through my jeans. This was revolting! But it was better than getting nabbed by the Mancatcher.

I gave up holding my breath and sucked in a load of fresh air. Well, "fresh" wasn't quite the word for it. Let's just say that if I didn't have to breathe, I would have quit right then.

It was hot in the dumpster. Not surprising— the thing was made of dark green metal. I began to feel like I was in a big, smelly oven. Sweat started pouring down my face.

How long was I going to have to stay here? When would it be safe to sneak out?

I heard the all-clear buzzer sound. Kids began to shout and laugh. No aliens after all!

I began to relax. Everyone would be inside soon. Maybe then I could get out of the dumpster or out of here without getting caught.

Unless, of course, the Mancatcher was still lurking around outside.

Soon I realized I was hungry. I also realized I was surrounded by food. I wondered if there was anything I could eat in here—maybe something that had just gotten thrown in.

If I have a good fairy, she has rotten timing. I can think of a dozen wishes I would rather have had come true that day, such as that I had never gotten out of bed to begin with that morning. No sooner had I started thinking about food than I heard a sound. Without thinking, I looked up just in time to see the round mouth of a garbage can being lifted over the edge of the dumpster. Down it came, right over my head—a garbage shower of soggy napkins, pickle bits, orange peels, ketchupy french fries, and who knows what else, all swimming in leftover chocolate milk.

I wanted to scream and shout, but of course then I would have been found and dragged off to the Mancatcher's office. My stomach was trying to add my own lunch to the pile of stuff in the dumpster, but I managed to hold things down.

I heard scraping noises. Another garbage can appeared above me. I scrambled back across the trash on my hands and knees. It was slick, and I had gone only a few feet when one hand plunged down into a soft spot and I dropped face first into the goop.

That was disgusting, but not terrifying.

What was terrifying was what I spotted only six inches in front of me as I was going down.

It was a hand. A human hand, lying between a ball of aluminum foil and a leaky, half-eaten jelly sandwich.

The garbage muffled my scream. When my heart stopped beating so fast, I lifted my head and looked again. That was when I realized the thing I had seen was more like a glove than a hand. A *skin* glove. Maybe a better way to describe it is to say it was like a mask for someone's hand.

It reminded me of Broxholm's mask—the one he had used to make him look human. When my brother had tried to fool me that morning, it was his human-looking arm that had tipped me off that he wasn't an alien. Until now, I hadn't thought about it the other way around. But since Broxholm was really green underneath his mask, then the rest of his skin must have been green, too.

Or maybe it wasn't. Who can tell with an alien? Maybe his different parts were all different colors. But whatever color they were, you can bet

his hands didn't look like human hands. So he must have been hiding them some way—*such as with a glove that looked like human skin.*

Only Broxholm had been gone since last May.

Everything in the dumpster had been put in over the last couple of days.

Which meant this glove was fresh garbage.

Which could mean only one thing.

We still had a teacher who was an alien.

CHAPTER FOUR

Honey Flint

The way I figured it, whoever owned the glove got left behind when Susan and the school band drove Broxholm out of town. But why hadn't the aliens come back for him? (Her? It?)

Had he/she/it been abandoned?

Or was the mission still on?

Whatever the case, I figured we had to do something about it. But first I had to get out of the dumpster. Except I was really afraid to do that, because if the alien, whoever it was, saw me climbing out, then he/she/it might wonder if I had found the glove. And in that case he/she/it might decide it was no good having me around.

I remembered the way Broxholm had fried the school door shut. Maybe I should just leave the glove where it was. But if I did, I couldn't prove what I had found. On the other hand (so to speak), if the alien somehow caught me with the glove, I was dead meat for sure.

I crawled farther into the dumpster to think. Settling onto a pile of used french fries, I stared at the glove, trying to decide what to do. The

21

only thing I knew for sure was that I didn't want to mess around with these guys!

After what seemed like hours the final bell rang. I could hear kids shouting and screaming as they ran out of the school. The back door scraped open. One of the janitors dumped more stuff into the dumpster.

By now my clothes were soaked with sweat—among other things. (At least I wasn't wearing nice new clothes, like most of the kids.) I would have traded almost anything for a breath of clean air. Closing my eyes, I leaned my head against the side of the dumpster. Ouch! The metal was hot. I scrambled over to the other side, the side in the shade, and tried again. That was better; not cool, but not burning, either.

I think I dozed off for a little while (who knows—maybe the fumes knocked me out). The next thing I knew, I was jolted awake by a horrible clanging noise. Someone was bouncing a basketball off the side of the dumpster! If I was into headbanger music, it would have been great. I'm not. It was terrible.

I heard another noise, and screamed as a huge rat scurried across my leg. Fortunately, my scream came at exactly the same moment as the next thump of the basketball, so I don't think anyone heard me.

"Get out of here!" I hissed at the rat.

It ignored me.

I grabbed a half-eaten apple and threw it as hard as I could. I missed, but the rat ran away—about a foot away. Then it went back to examining the garbage.

I decided if it left me alone, I would leave it alone. Except I found that whenever it got out of my sight, I started to feel nervous.

By the time the mad basketball player was done bouncing his ball off the dumpster, I felt like someone had been working over my head with a sledgehammer. I listened, which wasn't easy considering the way my ears were ringing. I couldn't tell for sure, but I thought the parking lot was empty.

I stared at the glove again and decided I had to take it with me. I knew that if I didn't, no one would believe me when I told them about it. And I had to tell people. If I didn't, who knew what the alien might do to our town?

Feeling nervous, I crawled to the front of the dumpster and poked my head above the edge. Fresh air! It was glorious. That was the single best breath I have ever taken.

It was also almost the last, since the next thing I saw was the Mancatcher. He was walking across the parking lot.

I dropped back into the dumpster and waited to hear the sound of his car pulling away before I tried again.

This time the coast was clear. Straining, I

pulled myself up on the edge of the dumpster. It wasn't easy—the heat had drained my strength. Finally I got my leg up over the edge and dropped back onto the loading dock. I felt as if there should be little odor lines in the air around me, like in the comic strips. I smelled worse than my brother's socks—which he usually wears for three days straight.

I was almost as confused as I was smelly. What should I do first? Who should I talk to about the hand mask I had found?

The answer to that one was simple. I had to talk to Susan. She would believe me.

But when I got to Susan's house and rang the bell, her mother opened the door. She took one sniff at me and told me to go home and get cleaned up. She wouldn't even tell Susan I was there.

So I didn't tell her that I was afraid to go home.

I was stinking my way down Pine Street, trying to figure out what to tell my mother, when a woman stepped out of the bushes.

I shoved my purple hand into my pocket. I didn't want anyone to see the evidence that I had pulled the fire alarm.

The woman was very pretty. She had long blond hair tied back in a ponytail and eyes as blue as my father's Buick. Her figure looked like someone had taken one of those Greek statues I like to look at in the encyclopedia and put clothes on it. A camera dangled from a strap around her neck.

"Hello, Duncan," she said, putting out her hand. "My name is Honey Flint."

I was dying to shake her hand, only I couldn't because I didn't want her to see the purple stain.

"How do you know who I am?" I asked.

She smiled, which probably should have been against the law since there wasn't much a guy could do to defend himself against it. "I've been paying attention," she said. Then she wrinkled her brow—and her nose—and added, "What happened to you?"

"I don't want to talk about it."

That wasn't really true. I did want to talk about it. But I was afraid she would laugh at me.

Honey shrugged. "I guess boys just have all kinds of adventures," she said. "Which is what I wanted to talk to you about. I understand you've had some adventures with an alien."

I felt a little prickle of fear. People in town had been keeping quiet about the alien situation. According to my dad, they figured no one would believe what had happened, so they just weren't talking about it. The police reports simply showed Peter as missing, either a runaway or a kidnap victim; they didn't mention anything about an alien.

So how did this woman know about what had happened? Was she one of the aliens? Did she know I had found the hand mask? Had she come to try to get it back from me?

"How do you know about the alien?" I asked nervously.

Honey smiled. "I have my sources," she said. Then she put her hand under my chin, so that I had to look up into those blue eyes, and said, "How would you like to be in the news, Duncan?"

"What news?" I asked, more interested now.

Honey smiled again. "The *National Sun!*"

Now *that* was exciting. My father loves the *Sun*. He makes my mother buy a copy every week when she does the grocery shopping. I like it, too. It has great headlines, things like "Elvis Ate My Baby" and "Walking Zombies Terrorize Town."

As soon as Honey mentioned the *Sun*, I felt I could trust her. I figured if she was an alien she would have said she worked for the *New York Times* or something. What kind of an alien would claim to work for the *National Sun?*

I also thought how amazed my father would be if his favorite paper did an article about me.

"Well?" asked Honey.

"Sure," I replied. "I'll talk to you. I like your paper. My whole family likes it. We keep it in the bathroom."

Honey blinked, then smiled and said, "Why

don't you just tell me what happened to you last spring?"

Then it hit me. Honey was my answer. This was what to do about the skin glove.

Reaching into my pocket, I said, "Honey, have I got a story for you!"

CHAPTER FIVE

How to Hide a Hand

My interview with Honey Flint went fine until I suddenly began to wonder if she was the alien after all. I mean, nothing said these guys were limited to one face. For all I knew, old Broxholm had carried a whole box full of masks, one for every occasion.

So when Honey asked if she could take the glove, I didn't know what to do. Maybe she had spotted me climbing out of the dumpster and was looking for a way to get the glove back without putting me on ice. (Not that I thought the aliens were kind and sweet or anything. But I could see where this one might not want to create more suspicion by having another kid disappear.)

Of course, if Honey was telling the truth about being a reporter, she might be able to help me convince the world that we still had an alien teacher in town. But if she was lying to me, if she was really the alien in disguise, then I would be handing over the only piece of evidence I had.

Finally I told Honey that she could take a photo of the glove. She seemed unhappy that she

28

couldn't have it, but I didn't know if that was because she was secretly the alien, or just because she wanted it to prove her story to her boss. (That's one problem when you start to get suspicious; you can't trust anything anymore.)

On the other hand, she did seem really thrilled with the story. "This is great," she kept saying. "Oh, Duncan, this is just great."

When we were finally done talking it was almost dark. Honey told me she would like to take me to get a milkshake or something, but that she didn't think any place would let us in the way I smelled, and she really didn't want to put me in her car, either. I suppose I should have been offended. But she said it real nice, and besides, it made sense.

I wasn't all that thrilled about walking home alone in the dark, especially since I was half expecting an alien to jump out of the bushes and grab me at any moment. Also, I didn't know what was going to happen to me when I got home. Being late wasn't a problem—my parents didn't really care that much what time I got there. But the garbage thing might be an issue.

Finally I stopped at old man Derwinkle's house. Mr. Derwinkle has the best lawn on the block, mostly because he's always watering it. I figured the odds were good that I would find a hose lying in the driveway.

I was right.

Old man Derwinkle is pretty deaf, so he didn't hear me spraying myself down. The first water was hot, from the hose lying in the sun all day. Once I got past the water that had been in the hose, the rest was cold. I didn't care; hot or cold, it all felt great. I didn't realize how much stuff had been stuck in my hair until I saw it coming out in the water that ran off my head.

So now my clothes were soaking wet, and stained in several places, but not nearly as smelly as they had been.

The same was true for me.

The only problem was that when I got home Patrick spotted me and bellowed, "Ma! Duncan's dripping all over the floor." So my mother made me go out back and take off all my clothes and put on a bathrobe before I could come inside.

Patrick snuck out back and took a picture of me while I was naked, which shows you what a booger he is.

I spent almost an hour that night trying to get the purple stain off my hand so I could go to school the next morning without getting in trouble. I wondered how long it would take to fade away. I considered asking Patrick, since he knows about this kind of stuff, but I couldn't count on him not to say something to my father.

Of course I could always stay home sick (I know four different ways to make myself throw up) or play hookey, but that's a little tricky the first couple of days of school. Later on, once you know the routine, it's different. But skipping at the beginning can really mess you up.

I suppose if I had been smarter I would have seen the answer sooner. It wasn't until I went back to my bedroom, which I have to share with Patrick-the-booger, that I thought of the alien glove. If it could hide the alien's hand, why not mine?

I pulled the glove out of my pocket and looked it over. What if it was full of alien germs or something? I decided to wait until morning to decide whether to use it.

When morning came my hand was as purple as ever. So I went into the bathroom, where no one would see me, and pulled on the glove.

It was like magic. The glove fit my hand perfectly, almost as if it was adjusting its shape while I was pulling it on. What was even weirder was that as I was putting it on, it changed color to match my other hand—as if it were a chameleon or something.

I had only two problems. First, the fingernails were too clean. So I grubbed them up a little. Second, there was a small hole at the end of one of the fingers. I suppose that's why the alien threw it away. I put a bandage over the hole. I have to wear a lot of bandages, so that looked pretty natural. Even so, if you had looked closely, you would have known it wasn't really my hand.

But unless you give them a reason to, most people don't look at stuff very carefully. That's one reason a guy like me can get away with a lot of things; people just don't see what you do.

My mother and father didn't notice my new hand at all. I didn't give Patrick a chance to see it.

I was really happy when I started off to school that morning. Things looked a lot better than they had the day before.

The Mancatcher was standing at the door when I came in. I knew he was looking for a kid with a purple hand, so I waved at him when I walked up.

"Hiya, Mr. Ketchum!" I said cheerfully.

He scowled at me. I knew he thought I was the one who had pulled the alarm. But when I waved my hand in front of him like that, it looked as if I had nothing to hide. So he didn't even bother to look at it closely.

Things would have been just fine if not for the fact that sometime during science class my fake hand started to fall apart. I tried to shove my hand into my desk, until I realized all we had were those stupid desks that have only a writing surface and no place underneath to keep stuff. I'm glad no one saw me flopping my hand around, trying to hide it in a space that wasn't there.

Finally I jammed my hand into my pocket. But

my pants were a little tight, so strings of flesh-colored material bunched up around my wrist.

I stared at them in horror.

Normally, I might just have been kind of upset. But I had spent a lot of time the night before thinking about who the alien might be. I had even asked Patrick which teachers were new to the school since last winter. I asked that because I figured that, like Broxholm, this alien would be someone who hadn't been around for a long time.

Patrick's response had been typical. "What do you care?" he snarled.

"Eat dog meat, fuzzhead," I replied.

I said that because if I told Patrick why I really wanted to know, or even let him think that it really mattered, he wouldn't tell me. This way he just punched me, and then told me what he knew.

As far as he could remember, our school had four new people. The first was none other than Manuel "the Mancatcher" Ketchum, who had started working there last January. The other three were teachers—Mr. Black, the math teacher; Betty Lou Karpou, who I had for home economics; and Andromeda Jones, the science teacher.

The same Andromeda Jones in whose class I was sitting at that very moment.

CHAPTER SIX

A Hand Out

I began to pluck at the strands of fleshlike stuff around my wrist, hoping I could get rid of them before the bell rang. I didn't have a chance to find out if I would have made it. Ten minutes before the period was over the phone on the wall started to buzz.

Ms. Jones picked it up. She listened for a moment, then turned to me and said, "It's for you, Duncan. You're wanted in Mr. Ketchum's office."

I swallowed. It wasn't that I had never been sent to the principal's office before. The secretary in our old school used to say that she saw more of me than she did of her own kids. She claimed that if I ever left for the junior high, she was going to have a special "Duncan Dougal Memorial Name Tag" put on the chair where I used to sit while I was waiting to see the principal.

Unfortunately, Mr. Ketchum was a lot tougher than our old principal. And he had already taken a dislike to me.

My plans for doing better this year were going down the toilet fast.

"Duncan," said Ms. Jones sharply, ' waiting for you!"

I sighed and stood up.

"Ee-yew," said the girl sitting next to me, when she saw the stuff around my wrist. "What's that?"

"Skin disease," I snapped. "But it's not catching, unless you get too close to it." Then I lurched toward her so I could watch her jump. I figured it was the last fun I would have that day. Maybe that week. Maybe forever, considering that Mr. Ketchum was one of the people on my alien suspect list.

As I walked out of the science room I wondered if I was being called to the office for the fake fire drill, because of the alien glove, or for some other reason altogether. More important, I wondered if I would ever leave Mr. Ketchum's office alive. It would be easy enough for him to do some alien nastiness to me and then claim that I had never showed up after he called for me.

Suddenly not showing up seemed like a good idea. I turned and headed for the back door of the school. I had only gone about four feet when I heard a deep voice say, "Thinking of leaving us, Mr. Dougal?"

I swallowed. Hard. Had the Mancatcher read my mind? Or did he just know the kind of thing I was apt to do? Either way, things were getting worse by the moment.

"Me? Leave?" I asked, trying to sound innocent. I turned to face him, then started a story about going to the bathroom before I came to the office. I could see by the look on his face that he knew it was baloney, that he knew I knew it was baloney, and that he knew I knew he knew.

So I shut up and followed him down the hall.

"Take your hand out of your pocket," he said once we were inside his office.

"I can't."

"Why not?"

"Skin disease," I said. "It's really awful. You don't want to see it."

The Mancatcher gave me a look of disgust. "I have a strong stomach. Take your hand out of your pocket."

"No!"

The Mancatcher looked frustrated. "All right, we'll come back to that. Right now I want to move on to other things. This morning I received a phone call from a woman named Honey Flint. Do you know her?"

I was so excited about the fact that Honey had called the school, I didn't stop to think. "Sure!" I blurted out. "I met her last night."

The Mancatcher nodded. "And when you met her, did you tell her about what happened here last spring?"

I nodded. I started feeling nervous again. Something was wrong, but I wasn't sure what.

Mr. Ketchum steepled his fingers in fro.
his face. His dark eyes glared at me. "That w.
a very foolish thing to do, Mr. Dougal."

Yikes. Was he mad because the school was trying to keep it a secret—or because he was the
alien?

"I've got a right to tell the truth," I said.

The Mancatcher laughed, as if the idea of me
telling the truth was too silly to even discuss.
"No one is questioning your right to tell the
truth, Mr. Dougal. What I want to know is if you
consider spinning some cockamamie story about
alien hand masks and an ongoing invasion part
of telling the truth!"

I got mad. "You call *this* cockamamie?" I
shouted, pulling my hand out of my pocket and
waving it in front of him.

"No," said Mr. Ketchum, "I call it purple ink,
the mark of a person who has pulled a false
alarm. Two false alarms in this case, since the
nonsense you spun out for that newspaper
woman counts as a false alarm as well."

I stared at my hand in horror. The glove was
gone; every last shred of it had disappeared. The
only thing left on my hand that didn't belong
there was the purple stain.

"Did you do that?" I asked, staring at the Mancatcher.

He looked at me in puzzlement. "Do what?"

"Make the glove disappear. You know it was

there. *You know it.*" I was shouting now, partly because I was frightened and partly because that's what I do when I get in trouble.

The Mancatcher stood up from behind his desk. "Settle down!" he said sharply.

"You leave me alone!" I shouted in terror.

"Duncan, *sit down!*" he bellowed.

I sat.

Then the talking started. First the Mancatcher lectured me about the danger of false alarms. Then a policeman came in and lectured me. Then a fireman came and did the same. By the time they were done we all knew that I was an antisocial jerk with no sense of responsibility and that I was probably going to wind up in prison.

By then I knew even better than they did how dangerous false alarms can be. Because of that stupid fire drill, no one was willing to believe me about the alien. Every time I tried to bring it up, Mr. Ketchum accused me of trying to take advantage of a "tragic situation" (meaning Peter's kidnapping) and told me to shut up.

Was he doing that because he didn't believe me—or because he was the alien?

After the police department and the fire department were done with me, Mr. Ketchum brought in my mother. Mom was crying, which I hate, and she asked me why I did it, which I couldn't really explain since I wasn't sure myself. Then she went on about how she didn't know what my father was going to do. I knew that was true. Based on past experience he would either beat me, or laugh and say, "Boys will be boys."

When they finally let me go I wasn't sure whether I should go home or run away. It would have been nice if I had had someone to talk to. But when you've been the class bully for several years, there aren't too many people who want to hear your problems.

I was walking down Pine Street, trying to figure out what to do, when I spotted Susan talking to Stacy Benoit and Mike Foran. It was like a little convention of good kids. I should have known I didn't belong there, but I tried to join the conversation anyway. (Stupid, right?)

"Hey, it's the Mad False Alarmer," said Mike when I walked up.

So I punched him in the nose.

Susan and Stacy were still yelling at me when I started to run. I didn't stop until I got home. I ran up the stairs and into my bedroom. But I couldn't cry because Patrick was there.

So I just lay in my bed, staring at the ceiling, wondering why I had been born.

CHAPTER SEVEN

Andromeda Jones

Even though I went to school every day, I didn't see the inside of a classroom again until the middle of the next week. That was because I had to sit in the Mancatcher's office for the next five days. The teachers sent down work for me, but I didn't understand it, so I don't know what the point was.

On Wednesday Mr. Ketchum decided he had had enough of me, and said I could start going to class again. Like it was a big gift or something.

He personally delivered me. I was hoping we would go during first period, so I could go to home economics. I didn't hate the class as much as I had expected to, and I really liked Miss Karpou, since she was a little goofy and made funny mistakes. I think she liked me, too, which was a nice change from most teachers, I want to tell you.

As things worked out, I had to wait until second period, because first period the Mancatcher was busy bawling out Orville Plumber. I thought this was pretty funny. Only I didn't laugh about it because if Orville had heard me, he would have plugged me good later.

"Ready for your grand return to society, Mr. Dougal?" asked the Mancatcher when he was done with Orville.

I nodded. The Mancatcher nodded back and gestured toward the door. I went out first.

When we got to science class, the teacher, Andromeda Jones, was getting ready to do a demonstration of static electricity.

"Now, class, I need a volunteer," she was saying as we walked in.

I had no intention of volunteering. After all, Ms. Jones was one of the new people to come on staff since last year, which meant that she was a prime candidate for being the alien. So who knew what that machine was really for?

Besides, I thought the way she dressed was silly. She wore a lot of that safari stuff—you know what I mean, khaki clothes with more pockets than an eighth grader has zits. I had heard a rumor that she claimed she dressed that way because teaching junior high was more dangerous than making a trek through the jungle, but I don't know if that was true or not.

Anyway, after about twenty seconds went by without anyone volunteering, the Mancatcher pushed me forward. "Duncan will be glad to participate in your demonstration, Ms. Jones," he said cheerfully.

"Not me! Uh-uh. No way."

The Mancatcher leaned down next to me and whispered, "Duncan, you haven't begun to learn how unpleasant I can be. Unless you want to spend the next five days in my office learning a new definition of misery, get up there and participate in this experiment."

I sighed and walked to the front of the room. People started to giggle and snicker, which only made things worse. I started to blush. It's just as well the Mancatcher was there. Otherwise I probably would have bopped someone.

"Listen up, everyone," said Ms. Jones. "The purpose of this demonstration is to give you an idea of how free-flowing electricity can affect things." She motioned to a black kid sitting in the second row and said, "Marcus, I want you to crank the generator."

Marcus smiled. "Sure thing, Ms. Jones."

I wasn't surprised that Marcus was smiling. One night last spring my father had gotten drunk and done some things that were pretty mean. I was still in a bad mood when I came to school the next day, and when Marcus had said something to me that I didn't like, I knocked him down and jumped on his lunch pail. So of course he was happy to crank the generator for Ms. Jones.

Once Marcus was in place, Ms. Jones put a huge helmet over my head. It was made of clear material, with a couple of jagged lightning bolts painted on the front. Lumpy knobs extended from the sides and the top.

Once the helmet was in place, Mr. Jones told Marcus to start cranking.

My scalp began to tingle. My hair started to move, as if a slight breeze were blowing through it.

Within a few seconds everybody was laughing like crazy. I suppose I did look pretty funny, with my eyes wide and my hair standing straight up.

Funny or not, I *hate* it when people laugh at me. I was so mad I wanted to bop someone. Only I couldn't, because the Mancatcher was right there.

So I held what I was feeling inside. But I had had it. Forget trying to save the world. For all I cared, the aliens could come and take everyone away.

Suddenly I stopped thinking about people laughing at me. Something else was going on, something weird. The *inside* of my head was starting to tingle. I felt like I had ants walking around inside my skull.

"All right, Marcus," said Ms. Jones. "That's enough."

Marcus gave the machine an extra crank or two for good measure.

"Marcus!" snapped Ms. Jones. "I want you to stop now!"

Looking like someone had just stolen his candy, Marcus stopped cranking. I promised myself I would bop him as soon as I got a chance.

The class was still laughing. My cheeks were burning as I headed for my seat.

I sat down and tried to listen, but my head was still tingling from the demonstration. I don't think they should be allowed to do things like that to kids.

After school I had an idea. That was kind of neat, since it didn't happen all that often. I decided I would go talk to Ms. Schwartz over at the elementary school. Since the alien had put her in a force field last spring, she might believe me when I told her about what I had found in the dumpster.

On the way, I saw a bunch of kids from the seventh grade standing in front of Sigel's Pharmacy. They were talking and muttering, but when they spotted me they began to hoot and holler.

Susan Simmons stepped out of the group and walked over to where I was standing. She poked her finger into my chest and said, "I knew you were a creep, Duncan, but even I never thought you would sink this low. I've met earthworms that I respect more than I do you."

I looked at her in shock. Now what had I done?

CHAPTER EIGHT

"Duncan Dougal, Boy Hero"

"Don't give me that look," said Susan.

"What look?"

"You know what I mean," she said. "Your 'What? Who, me? What did *I* do?' look. I've seen you use it on teachers a million times. All it means is that you're guilty."

Sheesh. You know you're in trouble when you can't even get a look on your face without people deciding you're guilty of something.

Before I could protest, Susan shoved a newspaper in front of my face. "Look at this!" she ordered.

I looked. I groaned. It was the *National Sun*. Across the top, in huge letters, it said, "TEEN HERO SAYS ALIENS STILL LURK IN SMALL TOWN!" Next to the headline was my picture.

"Listen to this," commanded Susan. " 'Duncan Dougal, the heroic teenager who foiled last spring's attempt by aliens to take over a typical American town, says that the entire planet remains in danger of an alien invasion.' "

"It's true!" I said.

"Oh, really?" said Susan. "*You* stopped the invasion? If I remember correctly, about the only thing you did was stand in front of Broxholm's viewer and scream."

I tried to explain that I meant it was true about the invasion. But before I could say anything Susan was quoting the newspaper again. " 'My friends were pretty scared last spring,' Dougal told *Sun* reporter Honey Flint. 'But I kept my cool. That's how I was able to figure out how to drive off the alien.' "

She looked at me. "*You* figured out how to drive off the alien?"

I blushed. Susan was the one who had done that, of course.

"Duncan Dougal, boy hero," called Stacy, her voice mocking.

"Oh, Duncan, save me!" shouted another girl.

"Shut up!" I yelled. "Just shut up, all of you!" Then I started to run.

What was I going to do? I knew one of our teachers was still an alien, but after Honey's article, there was no chance that anyone would believe me. I didn't mean to lie when I talked to Honey. I just tried to tell my side of things. I guess I got carried away.

"Duncan Dougal, boy hero!" The mocking words still rang in my ears as I raced through the front door of our house.

Patrick was already there. He was reading a

copy of the *Sun.* "Nice bunch of lies, buttface," he said when he saw me come in. "Your friends are going to love you for this one."

What friends? I thought miserably. *I don't have any friends.*

But I wasn't about to say that to Patrick. So I told him to shut up, and ran up the stairs into our room. I could hear him laughing downstairs.

It was even worse when my father came home and saw the paper. He was thrilled. He went out and bought twenty copies of the paper, and started calling all our relatives. It was the first time he ever acted like he was happy that I had been born, and it was all because of a bunch of lies I had told some stupid reporter.

Patrick was jealous about Dad being excited, so he spent the evening giving me noogies when no one was watching.

I had terrible dreams that night. People I knew kept turning into aliens. I woke up sweating and terrified.

I wanted to skip school the next day, but I didn't have a chance because my father insisted on driving me.

"I want to have a little talk with your principal," he said.

Actually, Dad's presence saved me for a little while. As we walked down the hall I could tell that kids were laughing. But with my father there, they didn't say anything out loud. They knew you didn't mess around with my dad.

Our visit to the principal's office was really embarrassing. We didn't see the Mancatcher, since my father insisted on going straight to Dr. Wilburn, the head principal.

"Look, what are you going to do about this alien situation?" asked Dad once the secretary had shown us in.

Dr. Wilburn was a tall, elegant woman with silver-gray hair. She looked at my father and said, "To tell you the truth, Mr. Dougal, we are still trying to decide. We had thought about suing Duncan for slander. However, since he is a minor we chose not to follow that option. I will be bringing the matter up at the Board of Education meeting later this week, where I will note your concern. An apology from Duncan would, of course, be useful."

My father looked like someone had smacked him in the face with a dead fish. When he demanded that Dr. Wilburn find the alien and get rid of him or her, Dr. Wilburn replied that there was no way the school was going to pay attention to the rantings of a disturbed seventh grader who had a long history of lying and was using last spring's tragedy to bring attention to himself.

"What about the glove?" demanded my father, his face red with anger.

Dr. Wilburn folded her hands in front of her.

"Show me the glove, and I will take action," she said.

"Duncan," said my father, "where's the glove?"

"It's gone," I whispered. "It fell apart."

The look on his face said it all. My father felt I had totally betrayed him.

Dr. Wilburn asked us to leave. Actually, she told us that if we didn't go, she would consider having us arrested.

I felt like a bug on the windshield of life. I felt like dog poop. I felt like blowing up the universe.

My father went off, and I went to my first-period class, which was home ec. I was looking forward to seeing Miss Karpou, since she was usually so cheerful, but she was all upset because the refrigerator was broken, and it had messed up her lesson plan for the day.

Plus, everyone started to laugh when I came in.

"Quiet, class!" said Miss Karpou.

No one paid any attention (which was what usually happened when poor Miss Karpou tried to get us to shut up). They just kept laughing and mocking me.

Too bad for them. Because a few hours later, when I finally got a clue as to who the alien was, I decided to keep it to myself.

Oh, I had my reasons. For one thing, I knew no one would believe me. For another, by then I didn't give a bat's butt about what happened to any of them anyway.

Besides, what gave me the clue was something so big, so tremendously exciting, that I knew it might be the most important discovery in the history of the planet.

Given the way everyone was treating me, I decided it was going to stay my secret.

CHAPTER NINE

How To Fry Your Brains

My discovery happened during math class. Mr. Black was explaining something about changing fractions into decimals, which was about the same thing as explaining how to make snoods into farfels as far as I was concerned, when suddenly I started to understand what he was talking about.

Now that may not seem like much to you. But it was the first time it had ever happened to me. I never got *anything* in math the first time around. Of course, I didn't usually listen real hard, but that was mostly because there didn't seem to be much point in listening, since I knew I wasn't going to get it anyway.

That day was different. As I listened to Mr. Black, all the things I was supposed to have been learning about math over the last eight years suddenly began to fit together. I was amazed. This stuff actually made sense! It connected. It was almost *beautiful,* in a weird sort of way.

My brain was tingling.

And then the next amazing thing happened.

Mr. Black asked a question, *and I knew the answer!* I thought about raising my hand, but that seemed too weird. Besides, if I answered the question, I knew people would just figure I was cheating somehow, and I had already had enough attention for one day.

It didn't take me too long to guess what was happening. Even a moron could have figured it out, and I was no moron—at least, not anymore.

It was simple: Andromeda Jones was the alien, and that machine she had used on me the day before was some sort of alien brain fryer—a brain fryer that made you smarter.

And if it could make me smarter once, maybe another dose would make me even smarter. Wouldn't that be cool? Forget Duncan Dougal, boy hero. I was going to be Duncan Dougal, boy *genius!*

I couldn't wait for the day to end. I had my plans already made. All I had to do was hang on and not bop anyone before the final bell rang. It wasn't easy, since I was still getting a lot of flak about the article in the *Sun.* But I didn't care anymore. I was going to be better than those jerks, better than all of the clods who had laughed at me all these years.

When the last bell rang I headed for the boys' room. I slipped into one of the toilet stalls and stood on the seat, so no one would see me if they looked underneath the door. Normally it wouldn't be a problem to stay after school; lots of kids stay after for different activities. But since I was known as a troublemaker, the school didn't want me around. If anyone spotted me, I would be sent home.

While I was standing there waiting, I found myself wishing that I had brought a book to read.

The very thought made me blink. Why in heaven's name would I want a book?

The answer was simple. My brain was hungry.

This being-smart thing was going to take some getting used to!

After about an hour I left the rest room. By that time most of the teachers had gone home, so I knew the halls would be a little safer. Besides, I was worried that one of the janitors would be coming in to clean the toilets before long.

How soon did I dare go use the brain fryer?

Not soon. The more I thought about it, the more I knew I didn't want to be interrupted. I didn't want any teachers or kids to catch me at this. It was going to stay my secret.

And I sure didn't want the alien to catch me.

Of course, the question I should have been asking myself was, why had she used it on me in the first place? I had probably gotten smart enough to think of that question. But I was too excited about the potential of all this to really worry about that idea. I didn't want anything to stop me—not even the possibility that this was a trap of some kind. If it was, the bait was worth it. I was tired of feeling stupid.

I began sneaking down the hall toward the science lab. I figured I might as well hide in there, even if I was going to wait until later to use the brain fryer.

After about three steps I decided to take off my sneakers, which aren't all that great for sneaking no matter what you call them. They're not bad, but they can give you a surprise squeak if you're not careful. Socks, even filthy ones, are quieter.

I heard a noise and scurried into a classroom. Lying on the floor, I watched as a whistling janitor pushed a broom down the hall. I tried to time him in my head and see how long it took before he came back. I counted a hundred and eighty elephants—about three minutes.

I decided to wait in right where I was, which was probably as safe as anywhere. Then I realized that I was across the hall from the library. That would be more interesting.

I waited for the janitor to go past again, then scurried across the hall and through the library door.

That was the first time I had been in the library this year. It might have been the first time in my *life* I had gone into a library without being forced. I found a book that looked interesting, something about cars, and crawled under a table in the corner.

I had enough light, but just barely. It didn't make that much difference. Even though I really wanted to read the book, I couldn't. I just couldn't figure out what the words said.

I had to get another zap of that brain fryer.

I tried to read for a little while longer. My eyes got heavy. My head sagged forward. Soon I was asleep.

When I woke the building was pitch dark. I crawled out from under the table and listened. Silence.

Well, near-silence. My stomach started to rumble, which wasn't surprising since I hadn't had anything to eat since lunchtime.

Trying to ignore my stomach's pleas for food, I stepped out into the hallway. It was kind of spooky being in the school all by myself. Kind of fun, too. Normally I might have decided that this was the time for a little mischief. Now I only had one thing on my mind: getting smarter.

Wow. Getting smarter in school. That was the first time the idea had ever occurred to me.

I tiptoed down the dark hall to the science lab. I paused at the door. The room was pitch dark. What if the alien was inside? For all I knew, she slept here—maybe she folded herself up and spent the night on the shelf. Who could tell with an alien?

My stomach rumbled again. I wondered if Ms.

Jones had anything to eat in the lab refrigerator. I figured if I was going to get smart, there was no point doing it on an empty stomach.

I felt my way to the lab refrigerator and pulled open the door. The little light inside seemed terribly bright after all the darkness. At first glance, it wasn't very encouraging. Most of the bottles had either little dead animals or small green plants. None of them looked like they were meant for human stomachs.

But at the back of the fridge I found a square Tupperware container that looked promising. I pulled it out. Hoping there would be something inside that might make my stomach stop complaining, I pulled off the lid.

Then I started to scream.

CHAPTER TEN

Poot!

I probably wouldn't have screamed if the stuff in the container had only been glowing. Even if it had only started to wobble, I might have been able to control myself, telling myself that I had accidentally shaken the container.

But when the glowing, jellylike mass I had uncovered began to ooze over the rim of the Tupperware and up along my arm, it was more than I could handle. I not only screamed, I dropped the container onto the counter.

But the blobby stuff was attached to me. It stretched, extending from my wrist to the container. I backed away, still screaming. The stuff continued to stretch, dragging the container with it. Suddenly the container slid off the edge of the counter. The goo inside pulled out with a horrible sucking sound, then snapped onto my hand, almost like a rubber band.

Then it started to whine.

"Aaaahh!" I screamed. "Aaah! Aaah! Get off! Get off!"

I shook my hand, trying to get rid of the glowing goo. The stuff stretched to the right, and then

to the left, bulging with my movements. Suddenly it came loose from my hand. It sailed through the air and landed on the counter with a *splat!*

It sat there whimpering for a minute. Then it slowly reshaped itself until it looked something like a two-foot-long slug. A glowing slug. The slug-thing lifted its front end (at least, I assume it was the front end) several inches into the air. It turned so that it was pointing at me.

And then it burped. It burped right at me, as if it wanted me to know how disgusted it was with me.

Then it collapsed onto the counter.

I wanted to run. But if I did, if I left that stuff lying on the counter, Ms. Jones would know that someone had been snooping around. And then I would never get to use the brain fryer. And I *wanted* to use it.

Suddenly I got an idea, which sort of shows you the effect the brain fryer had already had on me. The idea was this: if I used the brain fryer first, maybe it would zap up my mindpower enough so that I could figure out what to do with the slug next.

"You stay there," I said, pointing at the slug and trying to keep my voice from trembling.

It lifted one end and said, "Poot." But it said it in a kind of a weak little voice. I felt a twinge of fear. Did this thing have to be in the refrigerator to stay healthy? Was it going to die if I left it out on the counter? If it did, what then? Andromeda Jones would *know* that someone had been fooling around in the lab, and with her alien science it probably wouldn't take her long to figure out who it was.

Then another thought hit me. The worst one yet. What if I was *supposed* to come in here and fry my brains? And what if the reason was that this thing I had found in the refrigerator was some alien brain-eater that needed a supercharged brain for a snack every now and then, or else it would starve to death? Suddenly the phrase "brain food" took on a horrible new meaning.

I couldn't decide if I was glad I was smarter, because it let me think of things like this, or if I wished that I wasn't so smart, so such awful ideas wouldn't cross my mind.

Well, I had gone this far. No point in stopping now. Unless there was some way to put that machine in reverse, I was going to have to keep getting smarter just so I could stay alive.

Of course, none of this was going to make any difference if I couldn't find the thing. It suddenly occurred to me that maybe Ms. Jones had taken the machine home with her rather than leave it around in the school, where someone like me could get ahold of it.

That is, assuming she had a home, and wasn't curled up somewhere on a shelf in the science lab, just waiting for me to finish making a fool of myself by making a genius of myself so that she could feed me to the refrigerator slug.

I tried to remember what she had done with the machine after Marcus had finished cranking it the day before. At first I had no idea, which made sense, because I had been so mad at everyone that I wasn't really paying attention to what happened with the machine.

But then some images began to form in my head. I was remembering. I was *really* remembering! I hadn't even paid attention. But the images were stored in my brain.

I wondered how much else was stored in there.

This getting smart had its advantages after all!

I went to the walk-in closet where Ms. Jones had put the machine after her demonstration was over. My heart began to pound. What if she was inside waiting for me? My imagination created a vivid image of her hanging upside down from the ceiling, like some giant bat, just waiting for me to open the door so she could grab me.

I shook my head. I guess I was also getting more creative. Too bad courage wasn't also part of the package.

I was dying to turn on a light. But that was impossible. It would have been like standing on the roof and shouting that someone was snooping around in the building.

Taking a deep breath, I began to open the closet

door. Slowly. Very slowly, standing not in front of it but beside it, in case anything came charging out of the darkness.

Nothing. Silence.

Holding my breath, I began to peer around the edge of the door. Suddenly I felt something touch my ankle.

I learned it doesn't take brains to invent anti-gravity, just fear. I was halfway to the ceiling before my scream hit my lips. "Aaaaah!" I cried, just like before. "Aaaaahh!"

"Poot?" asked a small voice.

I was standing on the doorknob. I looked down and saw the glowing slug-thing on the floor beneath me. One end was lifted in the air, waving in a slow circle.

"Poot?" it asked again.

My heartbeat went from jackhammer level down to bass-drum level. For a moment I wondered what would happen if I jumped on the slug. Maybe I would kill it. Or maybe it would just split into a jillion little slime balls, each one of them hungry, angry, and out to eat my brain.

Scratch that idea.

"Go away!" I yelled.

"Poot!" answered the slug, sounding as angry as me.

I decided to take a chance. I jumped down from the doorknob, landing about two feet from the slug. "Scram!" I screamed.

"Poot!" it cried in panic. Then it formed itself into a circle and began to roll back across the floor to the lab table.

I didn't have much time. And after all that noise, there was no way I was going to sneak up on anyone (or anything) waiting in the closet. So I just walked in.

I didn't spend long looking for the thing. Actually, I didn't spend any time *looking* for it, since the closet was too dark inside to see anything. But I hadn't groped my way more than two feet past the door when I bumped into a rolling table, the kind teachers usually keep movie projectors on.

This one didn't have a projector; it had Ms. Jones's brain fryer.

Trembling with excitement, I rolled the machine back into the lab. Working in the dim light (half from the moon, half from street lamps) that came through the windows, I began to set up the machine. At one point I closed my eyes, trying to remember how the helmet had been connected to the generator. In a few seconds my brain sent me the image.

I smiled. This being smart was good stuff.

I looked around for the slug. It was lurking over by the lab table.

Placing the helmet carefully on my head, I got ready to fry my own brains.

CHAPTER ELEVEN

Zap!

I concentrated hard, trying to remember every-thing Ms. Jones had done that first time. After all, I sure didn't want to put the machine in reverse and make myself dumber.

Finally I was ready. Leaning one hand on the table next to the generator, I took the crank in my other hand and began to turn it—slowly at first, then faster and faster.

For a moment nothing seemed to happen. Then I felt a familiar sensation, as if a breeze were ruffling my hair.

I turned the crank a little faster.

My hair stood up. The ants started to crawl around inside my head.

I could almost feel myself getting smarter.

Now I started to really crank. "Come on, machine," I whispered, "come on, baby, do your stuff. Make me the next Einstein!"

Sparks of lightning began to flash through my head. Colors seemed to flicker around me. My hand was a blur as it turned the generator's crank faster and faster.

"Poot!" cried the slug-thing in alarm.

I thought I smelled something burning. I wanted to stop, but it was as if my hand were on automatic pilot, and my brains were too busy getting fried to give it a new order.

Z-A-A-A-P!

That sound, like an enormous spark sizzling through the night, is the last thing I remember. I blacked out and fell to the floor.

"Duncan," whispered a voice in my head. "Duncan, wake up."

I knew that voice; it belonged to weird Peter Thompson. But it couldn't be Peter. He was gone, off in space with Broxholm somewhere. Which meant that I had to be dreaming. Which meant that I was asleep.

I tried to wake up.

My body didn't cooperate.

All right—I'll stay asleep, I thought.

Peter's image materialized in my brain, looking just as he had the last time I had seen him, the night of our spring concert; the night Susan had used her piccolo to drive off the alien teacher.

It hadn't surprised me that Broxholm couldn't stand the sound of her piccolo. I didn't like it much myself.

But I had never quite gotten over the fact that as near as any of us could tell, Peter had *chosen* to go into space with the alien. I mean, the rest of us were terrified that we were going to get kidnapped. Old Peter couldn't wait to get his butt up into that spaceship.

Peter Thompson, tall and skinny, his brown eyes lost behind the thickest pair of glasses in the sixth grade.

"Duncan," he whispered again. "Do you remember how many times you beat me up in the last three years?"

I shook my head—in my dream, that is.

"Lots," said Peter with a nasty smile. Then his face began to change. His skin started to turn green: pale green first, then darker and darker, until it was the color of limes. His eyes stretched out until they looked like butterfly wings, huge and orange.

Broxholm!

"Get away from me!" I screamed.

And then I woke up—which didn't improve things any, because when I opened my eyes I saw myself staring back at me. Only my face had no color. No color at all, only a pale, greenish-yellow glow.

I blinked. The other me blinked, too.

I shouted in terror.

The other me said, "Poot!"

"Yeeaaah!" I cried, rolling away. It was the slug-thing. It had climbed/crawled/oozed its way to the underside of the lab table, where I had landed when I blacked out.

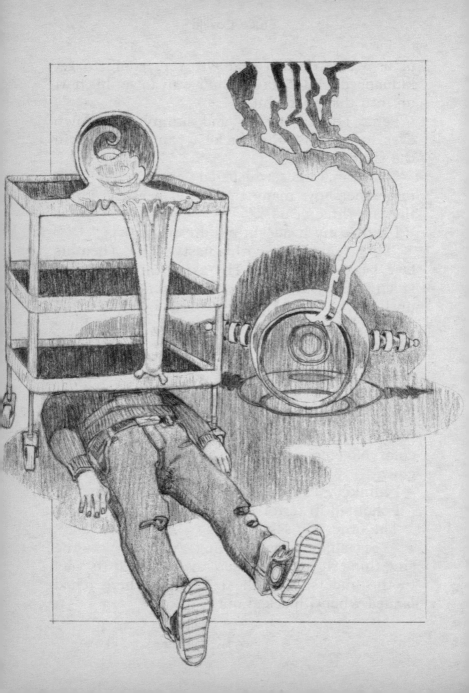

I didn't mind so much that it had been hanging over me, though that was pretty disgusting. What had me worried was the fact that it had imitated my face. I hoped it wouldn't do that when I wasn't around. It would be like an announcement that I had been here.

Could the slug only copy something that was in front of it? Or once it had copied something, would it be able to repeat that image over and over again? Who could tell? It's not like there's been a lot written about the mental ability of alien slugs that live in Tupperware containers kept in the refrigerators of junior-high science labs.

Of course, that was only one of the important questions I was facing at the moment. The others included (a) how was I going to get the slug back into the refrigerator? (b) how long had I been asleep? (c) had the brain fryer worked? (d) if it *had* worked, just how smart was I? and (e) what should I do next?

I decided the first thing to do was put the machine back. As I was packing it up I kept an eye out for the slug, which had crawled down from under the lab table and was watching me (I guess you could call it watching) from a spot on Andromeda Jones's desk.

"Stay there," I said, trying to sound menacing.

"Poot!" it replied.

I put everything back in place and rolled the

cart toward the storage area. As I closed the door, I wondered if the machine had some sort of meter that would let Andromeda Jones keep track of how much brainpower it had passed out. I figured I must have gotten smarter, since that wasn't the kind of thing I would have thought of before. Of course the thought didn't serve any purpose other than to make me nervous. But at least it showed I was thinking.

I also wondered if Ms. Jones had used the machine on anyone else.

And I wondered why she had used it on me. I didn't think it was out of the goodness of her alien heart.

That thought made me really nervous. It also convinced me that I had done the right thing. If Ms. Jones had fried my brains as part of some alien experiment, the best thing I could do to protect myself would be to get smarter as fast as I could.

I stopped and closed my eyes. How much smarter was I? It was hard to tell. I didn't really have any way to test it. And the last brain fry had taken a while to really have an effect. I did feel a tingling in my skull. Maybe the machine had stimulated my brain so that it was growing new synapses or something.

I blinked. Why in the world did I know a word like *synapses?*

Must be the brain fryer had worked after all.

Except I couldn't figure out where I had found the word to begin with. Was the thing putting new information into my head, like those subliminal messages in records that people keep worrying about?

I shivered.

"I'll think about it tomorrow," I said to myself. "Just like Scarlett O'Hara."

I blinked. It was happening again. Other than "Make my day," I had never quoted a movie or a book before. Where was this stuff coming from?

Never mind. I had to get out of the lab. No more fooling around. I grabbed the Tupperware container and its lid and headed for the slug.

"Inside!" I ordered, holding the container in front of it.

"Poot?" it replied, sounding pitiful.

"Inside!" I repeated, trying to sound fierce.

It made a little pooty sigh, then slumped forward and oozed into the container. I slipped on the cover, then sighed myself. Remembering how my mother used these things, I pressed the edges of the lid in place, then pushed down on the center to get rid of the extra air. This is called "burping" the Tupperware.

Only the sound that came out was a tiny "poot."

I put the container back into the refrigerator, which reminded me that I still hadn't had anything to eat.

Stomach rumbling, I stared around the room. As far as I could tell, everything was back in place.

Now to head for home, I thought. I decided to put on my sneakers. I figured that with the amount of screaming I had done already, if there had been anyone else in the building, they would have caught me by now anyway.

Even so, I walked quietly. Being alone at night in a building where you don't really belong will do that to you. Also, I still had a slight fear that the alien was going to jump out and nab me. That may not have made much sense, but you live through what I had lived through in the previous few days and tell me how much sense *you* make!

I went to one of the back doors, since I didn't want some late-night driver who happened to be passing by to spot me slipping out of the building.

The moon had disappeared behind a cloud. Its absence made the sky darker and the stars brighter. I looked up into the darkness and wondered which of those points of light Andromeda Jones called home. As I stood there staring into the night, I suddenly remembered that there was a constellation called Andromeda. Was that where she had gotten her fake human name? Pretty nervy of her.

Of course, it was pretty odd for *me* to remember the name of any constellation. But I barely noticed that fact. I guess I was already getting used to being smarter.

I walked around the school. The grass was soaked with dew, and so were my sneakers by the time I got to the front of the building. I could hear crickets singing in the distance.

I like being out in the night. The time is quiet and private, and you can feel more like yourself than you do in the daylight.

I heard the town clock begin to chime. Two hours past midnight. I figured I had better get moving.

I had only walked a couple of blocks when a car pulled up beside me and a deep voice said, "Get in, Duncan."

CHAPTER TWELVE

Accused

Once my heart started to beat again, I realized that I knew the person driving the car.

It was Peter Thompson's father.

"Get in," said Mr. Thompson again. "I'll give you a ride home."

I hesitated. Not because I didn't trust Mr. Thompson. I just didn't want to hear him whine on about how much he missed Peter now that he was gone.

On the other hand, I was tired and hungry, and getting a ride home instead of having to walk was very appealing. I decided I could listen to Mr. Thompson for a few minutes if it meant getting to my house—and my refrigerator—faster.

Actually, it was the refrigerator that was topmost in my mind. I was hoping I could find something in there that I could eat without having to worry about whether or not it was still alive. Of course, there was no guarantee on that matter. My father calls our refrigerator Resurrection City, because my mother puts in stuff that's dead and three months later takes it out covered with new life.

Whenever Dad says that my mother replies, "Look, Harold, if you don't like it, you can clean the refrigerator yourself, since last time I looked you didn't have two broken arms—though you might if you don't watch out."

Life at my house is not exactly like life on *Leave It to Beaver*.

"So, what are you doing out at this time of night?" I said as I climbed into the car.

The instant I said it I realized what a dumb question it was for a kid to ask an adult at two o'clock in the morning on a school night. But then, I've noticed that for most people, their tongue is the last part of their body to get smart.

I wished I hadn't asked. I wished it even more when Mr. Thompson answered, because depending on how I took it, what he said was either terribly sad or as scary as anything that had happened so far that night.

But I had asked, and Mr. Thompson answered.

"I'm looking for Peter," he said.

I closed my eyes. Even though my tongue was running ahead of my brain, I was smart enough to know that "Grow up, Jack, your kid took off for outer space because he couldn't stand you," was not the right thing to say under the circumstances.

Actually, I could think of several dozen things that were not the right thing to say under the circumstances. What I couldn't come up with was anything that I *should* say.

So I kept my mouth shut, which was probably the best proof I had had so far that the brain fryer was making me smarter.

"I know he's around here somewhere," said Mr. Thompson as he began to drive. "I just don't believe he's gone that far away. He's too smart to think he could survive someplace like New York City, even though he always wanted to live there."

This was sad. Mr. Thompson's idea of far away was several trillion miles short of where his kid had really gone.

"Do you know where he is, Duncan?" asked Mr. Thompson. "I know you were his best friend, because you were the only one who ever stayed overnight at the house. He must have told you where he was going. Tell me. Please tell me."

A car passed us, going in the other direction. In the glow of its headlights I could see that Mr. Thompson had tears running down his cheeks.

"Peter didn't like me as much as you think he did," I said truthfully, which was sort of a new experience. "He only let me stay at your place because I was in trouble."

Mr. Thompson nodded. "Peter would have done that," he said. "He was a good boy."

I felt like asking Mr. Thompson if he had ever bothered to tell Peter he thought he was a good kid while he was still around. I decided it wasn't the time.

I really didn't like seeing him so sad. So when he stopped the car in front of my house I said, "Listen, if I hear from Peter, I'll be sure to let you know."

"Thanks, Duncan," said Mr. Thompson. "You're a good boy, too."

I swallowed. My throat started to hurt. I don't know why, for sure, except that no one had ever said that to me before.

When I went inside everyone was asleep except Patrick, who was sitting up watching an old movie. "Ma's mad 'cause you didn't call," he said.

I nodded. She always said she was mad when Patrick didn't show up, too. But usually she was really just relieved.

I went upstairs and got into bed.

But I didn't go to sleep.

Mostly I stared at the ceiling, trying to figure out the answers to questions I had never asked before I got so smart.

If I didn't know how to take Mr. Thompson, my teachers began having the same problem with me. It started two days after I gave myself the second dose of the brain zapper. Mr. Black, the math teacher, called me in at lunchtime and said, "Mr. Dougal, I am going to give you one chance to confess. Otherwise you will be going straight to the principal's office."

I looked at him. "Confess to what?" I asked.

He glared at me. "Mr. Dougal, I cannot abide cheating. I want to know how you passed the math test I gave you yesterday afternoon."

Sheesh! What was I going to tell him? That I passed it because I had gotten my brain fried and I was probably smarter than he was? I was smart enough to know that was a bad idea, even if I hadn't been smart enough to realize that suddenly passing a test was going to get me into trouble.

I closed my eyes and thought fast. "I'm turning over a new leaf," I said, trying to sound sincere. "I really studied for that test."

Actually, that was a lie. I had barely studied at all. I didn't need to; my brain had just absorbed the information.

From the look on his face, Mr. Black might have found the fried-brain story more believable.

"I want the truth," he said.

"Mr. Black, I didn't cheat. I can prove it. Give me some more questions, right now, and I'll do them for you. You'll see. I really know the stuff. I do!"

Mr. Black smiled, as if he knew I had really gotten in over my head. "All right," he said. "Have a seat."

I sat down in the first row. Mr. Black went to

his desk and took out a sheet of paper and a pencil. He scribbled down a few numbers, then brought the paper over and set it in front of me.

I wanted to kick him. The problem he had written down was harder than anything on the test. He *wanted* me to get it wrong.

Brain, I thought, *don't fail me now.*

CHAPTER THIRTEEN

The Sound of Music

I stared at the problem. For a moment my mind seemed to go blank. Then I could almost feel the ants start crawling around inside my head. Without looking up, I reached for the pencil Mr. Black was holding. He handed it to me, and I began to figure.

Thirty seconds later I had the answer.

When I handed the paper to Mr. Black he was staring at me as if I had just sprouted wings and flown around the room a couple of times.

"How did you do that?" he asked.

"Must be you're a great teacher," I said. It was a nasty crack, but I was really mad.

Mr. Black sat down at his desk. He looked at me, at the paper, and then back at me. "You can go, Duncan," he said at last. "Please keep up the good work."

I should have learned my lesson from that little scene. People don't want you to change too fast. Some people don't want you to change at all, because then they have to think when they deal with you.

But I was too excited about my new brain to hide my light under a bushel for the moment. When I left Mr. Black's room I went straight to the library.

The librarian looked at me suspiciously. "We don't circulate the swimsuit issue of *Sports Illustrated*, Duncan," she said when I walked through the door.

"That's all right," I said. "I want to read a book."

The look on her face was even better than the one on Mr. Black's had been.

It wasn't until I got to science the next morning that I realized I had better be careful about this. Home economics had been fun. Even though I was doing better there, people just figured it was because I had settled down for a couple of days. No one thought that much of my intelligence because I didn't ruin the eggplant, though Miss Karpou gave me a big smile and thanked me for my good work, which made me feel kind of warm inside.

But when I sat down in science class it suddenly occurred to me that if I showed off too much, Ms. Jones would be bound to know what I had been up to.

On the other hand, since she was the one who had fried my brains in the first place, I shouldn't have to act entirely stupid in her class, either.

The ones who really had a problem coping with

me were the other smart kids. They had known me as Duncan the Dunce for so long that they didn't know how to react when I started answering questions that some of them couldn't figure out.

Part of the reason I was getting smarter so fast was that I was reading my brains out. Or in. Or something. It only took me a day or two to realize I needed to do that in secret. The first time Patrick saw me reading a book he pulled it out of my hand and asked me if I was turning into a geekoid. I couldn't believe he could be such a jerk.

Then I remembered how I used to treat Peter Thompson.

My father was no better. He told me he thought reading was a complete waste of time.

So I had to do all my reading where no one could see me.

Two nights later I stayed after school and gave myself a third zap with the brain fryer. I looked in the refrigerator for the slug-thing, but it was gone. I wondered if Ms. Jones had eaten it or something. To my surprise, the idea made me a little unhappy. Despite the fact that it had terrified me, I had gotten kind of used to the little guy.

Between the third session with the brain fryer and the fact that I was reading hundreds of pages a day, I could feel myself getting smarter faster and faster. Something I hadn't expected was that the more I learned, the more things made sense. Sometimes learning one thing made three other things suddenly come into focus. I was starting to find the connections that made learning fun.

Sheesh. Listen to me! Who ever thought I would use the words *learning* and *fun* in the same sentence?

Even though I was having fun, there were a few things still bothering me. Number one was the question of what Andromeda Jones was up to. Why had she fried my brains to begin with? And why hadn't she said or done anything about it since? Was I some kind of experiment? Had the aliens gotten together and said, "Hey, let's see what happens if we make a bozo bright"? I didn't particularly like that idea, though from my point of view it was working out OK for the time being.

But what if when the experiment was over she decided to take the smartness back? That was the most frightening idea of all. I didn't think I could stand going back to being what I used to be.

The second thing bothering me was the way the other kids were acting. No one knew what to think about me anymore. The only one who didn't treat me like a complete freak was Susan.

My third problem was that I was getting so smart that *I* didn't know what to do about it. If a kid like me, or like I had been, suddenly announced that he had figured out how to create world peace, would you pay any attention to him? More important, would the President and Congress? But that was exactly the situation I found myself in.

When I described a brilliant plan to end world hunger, my social studies teacher said it was silly.

The next day I figured out cold fusion—only I didn't dare tell *that* to my science teacher, since I didn't want her to know I had been tampering with her brain zapper.

But can you imagine how frustrating it was? Think about it. Wrapped inside my magnificent brain was information that would have solved every one of earth's energy problems, eliminated most of our pollution problems, and made me a billionaire in the process. And there wasn't a darn thing I could do about it!

I tried. I even sent a letter to the Department of Energy telling them I would *give* them the information. They sent back a very polite note letting me know in the nicest possible terms that they thought I was an idiot.

That was one more thing I learned once I got smart: no one wants to listen to a kid with an idea. Sometimes I thought I could understand why old Peter had decided to go with Broxholm that night.

Even so, I was feeling pretty good about myself, and about what had happened—until the night that I went to bed and couldn't get to sleep because of the radio.

At least, I thought it was the radio.

"Come on, Patrick," I said. "Turn it off so I can go to sleep."

"Turn what off?"

"Your radio!"

"My radio is broken, Duncan Dootbrain, so shut up and leave me alone."

I blinked. Patrick was telling the truth. I remembered hearing him complain to my mother the day before about his radio being broken.

So where was the music coming from?

I rolled over, and the station changed. Instead of Madonna, I was getting a blast of Beethoven. I rolled back, and Madonna's voice came back on.

Or maybe I should say back in. Because what I had figured out was this: the music was inside my head.

Most people have five senses. Suddenly I had six. I had fried my brain one time too many, and turned it into a radio receiver.

CHAPTER FOURTEEN

Invisible Information

I didn't get much sleep that night. Every time I moved my head I got a different kind of music playing inside it.

Finally I found a station that played truly boring elevator music that should have put me to sleep almost instantly. It probably would have, if I hadn't been so terrified about what I had done to myself.

Lying in bed while elevator music plays endlessly in your head and you sweat with fear about what you've done to yourself—that's about as bad as life can get.

At least, that was what I thought at the time. The next day I realized that I was wrong.

I had forgotten about TV.

It started shortly after home economics class, when I closed my eyes and found myself watching a rerun of *The Donna Reed Show*.

You might think having a TV receiver in your brain sounds like fun. Believe me, it's not. For one thing, I couldn't turn it off. The shows were always there. If you think about how smart I had become, and how stupid most television is, you'll see how painful this was for me.

I had read enough by this time to guess what was going on. To understand, you have to start by realizing that the air around us is filled with invisible information. That may seem weird, but it's true. Think about it for a moment. Whenever you smell something, you're pulling information out of the air. When you hear something, you're pulling information out of the air. What are you smelling? What are you hearing? You may be able to see the object, but you can't see the smell itself; it travels to you in the form of incredibly tiny molecules. The sound comes to you in waves of vibrations moving through the air.

Invisible information.

The thing is, we know how to interpret that information. Our noses and our ears take the molecules or the sound waves and translate them so that we can say, "Ah, rotting fish" or "squealing tires."

Now, we know that we don't take in all the information around us. For example, our noses aren't built to process smells the way a bloodhound's can. When a bloodhound tracks someone down by following their smell it's using invisible information we could use, too, if only we could perceive it.

Now think about your radio. You turn it on, and you get instant music. (Or news, or idiotic disk jockey chatter, or whatever.) Where is the music coming from? Inside the radio? That would be true if you were playing a tape or a compact disc. But when you turn on the radio, it pulls the music out of the air.

The music was there all along; you just couldn't get at it.

The same is true for the TV set. You turn it on, and bang! sound and pictures both. And where are they coming from? Unless you're playing your VCR, they're coming from radio waves that the television pulls out of the air.

Those same kind of waves are passing through your head all the time. Right now, even as you read these words, an incredible amount of information is passing *right through your skull.* Broadcast waves from four or five television stations. A dozen kinds of music. News reports, police calls, CB radio chatter—they're all passing through your brain *right now!* If you could perceive them, if your brain could interpret them the same way it does sights and sounds and smells, then you could pull that information right out of the air. It's there; your brain just doesn't know how to find it.

My ultra-powerful brain had learned how to receive that information.

The problem was, I couldn't turn it off.

What made things worse was that I couldn't sort it out. The images all blurred together. When

I closed my eyes I might hear two or three radio stations while I watched Scooby Doo chase Pee-wee Herman across the bridge of the starship Enterprise.

I figured another day or two of this and I would go mad. As it was, I couldn't think. The reputation I had started to get for being smart was going to dissolve pretty fast. People had spent years thinking of me as stupid and a couple of weeks thinking of me as smart. If it all ended now, they would figure the smart thing had been just a mistake. It wouldn't take long for them to forget it altogether.

I had had my temper under control for the last several days. But with all this going on in my head, with the constant noise and confusion and my own terror at what I had done to myself, I wasn't able to control things as well. So that afternoon, when Mr. Black asked me the kind of question I should have been able to answer in a flash, I couldn't come near the solution.

"Come, come, Duncan," he said. "Pay attention. You know what this is all about."

"How do you know what I know?" I shouted. "Until two weeks ago you thought I was I total jerk."

Mr. Black was so surprised he dropped his chalk. It shattered into a dozen pieces.

I closed my eyes, waiting for him to tell me to go see the Mancatcher.

To my surprise, he said, "Are you feeling all right, Duncan? Would you like to see the nurse?"

I blinked. There was something important going on here. But between the fact that my head was picking up *The Dating Game* and a violin concerto by Mozart, I couldn't quite figure it out.

"Duncan, I asked if you want to see the nurse."

I shook my head. I didn't think the nurse could help. An electrician might do me some good, if he or she could install an on/off switch and a volume knob somewhere on the back of my neck.

"I'll be all right," I muttered, which was the first lie I had told in several days. "Sorry I yelled."

Mr. Black shrugged. "Sometimes these things happen."

I lost my temper again that night at home, when Patrick said, "Hey, Duncan, how come you don't have your nose stuck in a book tonight? Decide to get normal for a while?"

I told him to shut up. He hit me in the head.

I announced that I had had enough of him, and I was going to run away from home. I didn't mean it, of course. But when things get this way, sometimes you say things you don't mean.

I hadn't had a good night's sleep since this started. That night, when I lay down in bed and closed my eyes, I saw Humphrey Bogart kissing John Wayne's horse while Ed McMahon was trying to sell dog food to Attila the Hun. In the background I was getting a mixture of Lawrence Welk and a rap group called Stinking Pond Scum.

I thought I was going to scream.

Then it all disappeared.

"Duncan," said a voice in my head. "Duncan, can you hear me?"

It was Peter Thompson!

"I can hear you," I whispered.

"Duncan," he repeated. "Can you hear me?"

He sounded desperate.

"Where are you?" I whispered. But he was gone. The radio and the TV programs came pouring back into my head.

I wondered if I was losing my mind. I had to talk to someone. I wished I could call Susan. But it was too late; her family would be asleep, and her parents would never put her on the line at that hour.

I got up and wrote her a note: "Susan, I have to talk to you. This is *urgent!* I am sorry about the *National Sun* article and everything else. Please, *please* talk to me today after school. Duncan."

The next morning I stuffed the note in her locker.

That day was the worst yet. I couldn't concentrate at all. I broke a bowl in home economics, and then yelled at Miss Karpou when she tried to ask if I was all right. I felt terrible.

I felt even worse when I found out that Susan was home sick that day. Now what was I going to do? I *had* to talk to someone.

Finally I asked Miss Karpou if I could see her after school. I didn't really think she could help me; she was too ditzy. But she might be able to think of someone who could help me. And I had a feeling that at least she would believe me.

After the last bell I went to Miss Karpou's room. She was fiddling around with something in the test kitchen when I got there. That was fine; that area was really private, and I didn't want anyone to overhear us. Especially not Andromeda Jones.

Miss Karpou looked up when she heard me come in. "Hello, Duncan," she called cheerfully. "Come on back."

I closed the door and walked back to where she was working, trying to shut out the whining violin music that was running through my head.

"I'm sorry about yelling this morning," I said once I was standing next to her.

Miss Karpou shook her head. "Don't worry about it, Duncan. I didn't take it personally."

I tried to smile. If only the violins would shut up!

"Miss Karpou," I said, trying not to cry, "I have to talk to someone. I have to tell someone what's happening to me. Only it's so unbelievable, I'm afraid you're going to think I'm crazy."

She shook her head. "I'll believe you, Duncan. I promise."

Then she pointed her wooden spoon at me and twisted the handle. My body seemed to lock in place.

How could I have been so stupid? I thought.

Frozen not with fear, but by some alien technology, I watched in horror as ditzy little Betty Lou Karpou grabbed her chin and began to peel off her face.

CHAPTER FIFTEEN

No Secrets

Miss Karpou's real face didn't look anything like Broxholm's. Her skin was a soft green-gold color—about the shade of willow trees in spring. It was also covered with scales. She had three eyes, with the one in the middle being located above the other two, sort of in the center of her forehead. It was the biggest of the three. I didn't realize about the third eye right away, since it was hidden under a protective patch.

"Ah, that feels better," she said as she pulled the patch away. The third eye opened. Its purple pupil was vertical, like a cat's. When it focused on me I wanted to shout. I wanted to run. I wanted to faint.

But I just stood there, frozen and forced to watch.

The strangest part was yet to come, for once Miss Karpou had removed the patch from her eye, she pulled something that was a little like a hair clip away from her nose.

"Ohhhh," she sighed, as her nose rolled down, "and isn't *that* a relief."

I could see where it would be, if you had a nose like hers. It looked like it belonged to a little green elephant. Only Miss Karpou's nose was flatter than an elephant's. Also, it had three prongs (or fingers, or something) on the end. When it was resting it dangled down to cover her mouth. But it wasn't resting very often. Mostly it was waving around in front of her, like some sort of snake with a mind of its own.

"Oh, Duncan, you can't imagine how good it feels to really let my hair down," she said as she pulled off a thing that had covered her head like a shower cap.

"Let my hair down" was the wrong phrase, since most of it stood straight up as soon as she pulled off the cap. I don't know if it really qualified as hair. It was lavender, and thick as worms. Like her nose, it seemed to move on its own, each thick strand going its own way, curling, uncurling, bending from side to side.

Watching it gave me the willies. Unfortunately, I couldn't close my eyes.

"One last thing, and then we can talk," she said. "Or at least, I can talk. You'll just have to listen for a while."

She turned to the refrigerator and pulled out a familiar-looking piece of Tupperware. Lifting off the top, she said, "You can come out now, Poot."

She turned the container on its side. The glowing slug-thing oozed over the edge and onto the counter.

I figured this was either good news or bad news. If this was the same slug I had first met, it was good news, because I was glad it was still alive. If it was just an after-school snack for Miss Karpou, that was bad news, because I really didn't want to watch her eat the thing.

After a few seconds she put her hand on the counter. The thing began to ooze its way up her arm. I figured that unless she ate with her armpit, this was a good sign.

"Well, now that I'm comfortable, let's see what we can do about you," said the alien.

She started to walk in my direction. I wanted to scream and run, but I was still frozen. I couldn't even make my eyes go wide in horror, though they were trying for all they were worth.

The alien touched me on the forehead with her wooden spoon. Then she pushed until I fell backward. I had a moment of total terror, almost worse than when she had started to take off her mask. Maybe falling backward is some basic fear built into our genes. It sure felt that way.

But I didn't fall very far, because my forehead was still connected to her wooden spoon. She made a couple of adjustments to the spoon, and soon my body was stretched out flat in the air, three feet above the floor. When she lifted the spoon I came with it, as if I weighed no more than a balloon.

Using the spoon, Miss Karpou put me on the countertop. Then she bent down and looked me in the face. The slug oozed along her arm, as if it wanted to get a closer look, too.

It was bad enough to have the alien's three eyes staring into my two. But when her nose started examining me as well, poking and prodding around my face as if it was gathering information for its own purposes, I really, really wanted to scream—especially when one of those green feelers on the end of the alien's trunk poked its way into my right nostril.

"Had a rough week, Duncan?" asked the alien in a voice that actually sounded sympathetic.

What was I supposed to do? Nod and smile at her? I did the only thing I could do, which was lie there and stare straight up with wide eyes.

If only the violins inside my head would shut up so that I could think!

"Poor Duncan," said Miss Karpou. "Let's see if we can't improve your situation a little."

She went to the cupboard where we kept the mixing bowls. Stretching her arm, she took one down from the top shelf. When I say stretching her arm, I don't mean like you or I would stretch. Her arm actually got longer, as if it were made of rubber or something.

The mixing bowl looked like the bowls we

used almost every day in class. But it must have been filled with some kind of alien circuitry, because when she sat it on edge on the counter and then slid my head inside, it blocked out the radio reception.

What bliss! For the first time in days I had silence inside my head. That was such a relief I could have kissed that hideous alien face.

"My face is not considered hideous where I come from," said Miss Karpou. "And I would not want a kiss from you anyway."

I would have blinked in surprise if I could have. (Actually, I would have jumped off the counter and run like hell if I could have, but that wasn't even a possibility.) Had she just read my mind?

"Yes," said Miss Karpou.

She *had* read my mind!

"It's not quite mind reading," she said quietly. "The circuits in the mixing bowl are not only blocking the radio and television waves coming into your brain, they are amplifying and sorting the waves that you create within. Sorting is the big problem, of course, since your brain is doing a multitude of things at once. The task for the machine is to choose the brain patterns that are relevant, sort them into some sort of order, magnify them, and transmit them to the receiver plugged into my head. It's *like* mind reading, but it's all done with machines."

What was I supposed to say to that?

"Don't say anything. I'll do the talking. But since we are going to be working together, we might as well get to know each other a little better."

Working together? I thought in alarm.

The alien smiled. "I need your brain," she said cheerfully, just before she put me to sleep.

CHAPTER SIXTEEN

Kreeblim

When I woke up again, I was in the alien's home. I don't remember going to sleep, so I assume she knocked me out before she took me there.

I have no idea how she got me out of the school. Lifting me was no problem, of course, since that wooden-spoon thing of hers had some kind of built-in antigravity device. But I'm not sure how she managed to get me to her car without anyone seeing. Maybe she put me in a big box. Maybe she shrank me and carried me out in her pocket. Heck, for all I know, she used some kind of alien fax machine to disassemble my molecules, then sent me over the phone lines. Who knew what these people could do?

Anyway, when I opened my eyes again, I was in a living room. Just a normal living room. It wasn't bare, like Broxholm's had been, and it wasn't filled with weird alien furniture, either. It was just a room. The alien was sitting in a kind of beat-up-looking armchair, looking all green and scaly. She was wearing faded jeans and a blue

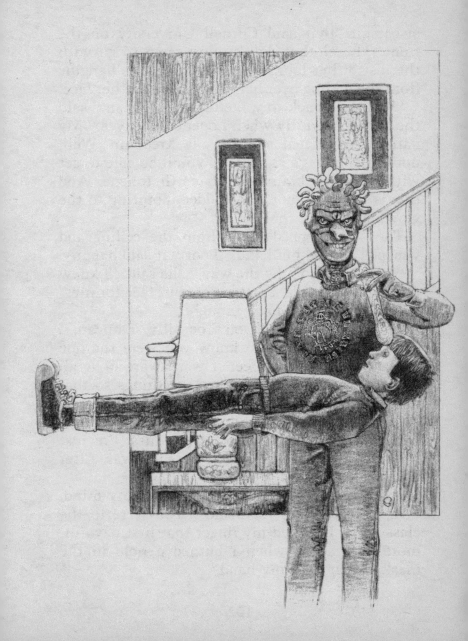

sweatshirt that said Cornell University on the front. The clothes didn't quite seem to go with the rest of her look. The slug-thing was hanging from the ceiling over her head, imitating her face.

"Welcome back to wakefulness, Duncan," said the alien cheerfully when I opened my eyes. "My name . . . my real name . . . is Kreeblim. Well, not quite, but it's as close as you'll be able to get with an earth brain and an earth tongue. And this is my pet, Poot," she added, pointing to the glowing blob on the ceiling.

The slug dropped down from the ceiling and wrapped around her hand. "Poot!" it said happily.

"Poot likes you, by the way," she said. "I knew that when it made a picture of your face for me."

Poot is a tattletale! I thought.

Kreeblim smiled. "Don't be silly, Duncan. I didn't need the poot to know you were the one using the mind enhancer. I was aware of it all along. Actually, I tried to arrange things so that it would be you, since you were one of the few kids in the school whom I could borrow for a while without causing too much fuss. I'm just surprised you hadn't figured out who *I* was. After all, you had clues."

She must have read the question in my mind. "Oh, come, come," she said. "You were in the class when I burned my finger that first day—or, more accurately, when I burned a hole in the mask I wear over my hand."

I wanted to groan, only I couldn't on account of being frozen, or whatever it was she had done to me. Why hadn't I realized what was going on? Of course, the fact that I had found Poot in the science-lab refrigerator and not in the home ec room had helped throw me off track.

"Ah, yes," said Kreeblim, reading my mind again. "But if you'll think back, you'll remember that you found the poot shortly after the refrigerator in the home economics room had broken down. I had stored the poor baby in Andromeda Jones's lab for safekeeping until my refrigerator was fixed."

I remembered how Poot had been missing the next time I snuck into the lab; another clue I had ignored.

"Don't be angry with yourself, Duncan," said the alien.

But I should have figured it out! I thought fiercely.

Kreeblim laughed. "You had a lot of other things on your mind," she said. "And you certainly didn't have a lot of experience in using that newly enhanced brain of yours. However, I *do* have a real use for it—which is why I brought you here."

That sentence had more possible meanings than I wanted to consider at the moment. On the other hand, my increased intelligence had stuck me with an incurable curiosity. *What are you going to do with me?* I thought, despite the fact that I wasn't at all sure I wanted to know.

"I need you for communication purposes," said Kreeblim. As she spoke, one of her lavender hairs made the mistake of prodding the poot. The slug seemed to absorb the end of the hair, which squeaked and pulled back in surprise, slightly shorter than it had been.

Kreeblim patted her head, and the hairs all bent away from Poot and started waving in the opposite direction. She turned her attention back to me. "You see, when your friend Susan forced Broxholm into an emergency retreat, it left me stranded here. Normally he would have come back for me fairly quickly. However, her interference created a slight crisis, and he received an emergency call to return to our home base.

"Even that wouldn't have been so bad, except for the fact that it left me without some of my basic equipment. The worst loss was my communication device. I'm sure you've read enough by now to know how fast light travels."

A hundred and eighty-six thousand miles per second, or about five-point-eight trillion miles a year, said my brain, supplying the information without me even having to look for it.

Kreeblim nodded. "And you also know that even that incredible speed is inadequate for talking across the vastness of space."

I would have nodded back, but being frozen sort of limits your nonverbal responses.

"What you probably don't know," continued Kreeblim, "is that we have developed a few ways around that kind of limitation. However, I don't have the hardware to replace my trans-space radio device. So I have to use you instead."

She smiled. "That, dear Duncan, is why I arranged for you to be connected to the brain enhancer. I needed someone to act as a communication center for me, and you seemed the most likely candidate. It was almost more than I could have hoped for when you started giving *yourself* treatments, since it meant I could delay the time when I needed to bring you here—which would also delay any fuss that might be caused by your disappearance."

When she said that I felt a little surge of hope. Sooner or later someone was going to miss me and start looking for me. I tried to clamp down on that idea, but thoughts are hard to control.

Kreeblim sighed, almost as if she felt sorry for me. "Don't waste your emotional energy thinking someone is going to come and rescue you," she said. "After all, just last night you told your family you were going to run away from home. So no one is going to be all that surprised when you don't show up for the next few days. And by the time they decide to look for you, it won't make any difference."

"Poot!" said the slug on her shoulder.

CHAPTER SEVENTEEN

Forced Into the Field

Something started to beep upstairs. Kreeblim kept her right and left eyes fixed on me while she rolled the center one toward the sound.

"I need to go tend to something," she said with a slight sigh. "I'll be back soon. We can talk some more then."

You call this talking? I thought bitterly.

Kreeblim made a clicking noise with her tongue. "Come, come, Duncan. Whether or not you are actually opening your mouth, we are exchanging ideas, which is what talking is all about. I'm sorry my language implant does not have a word adequate to describe the fact that your half of the conversation comes in thoughts rather than words. I rather suspect, however, that the problem has more to do with a lack in your language than in the device itself."

The beeping upstairs continued. She turned and left the room.

While she was gone I tried to move. I strained as if I were trying to lift an elephant—and with about as much effect. I wasn't cold, but I was frozen stiff as a popsicle. As I stood there, paralyzed, in the middle of the living room of an alien invader who happened to be masquerading as a slightly dippy home economics teacher, I decided that life is just so fascinating I can barely stand it.

The poot came over and rolled around my feet for a while. Then it started to climb my leg. That's when I knew that whatever Kreeblim had done to paralyze me was foolproof. I couldn't even shudder!

The poot kept climbing until it reached my shoulder, where it settled down like a small kitten. Even though I kind of liked the poot, I couldn't quite convince myself that it wasn't about to make itself real thin so it could ooze into my ear canal and suck out my fried brain.

Suddenly it reached up with a blob of itself—a pseudopod, my brain informed me, even though I hadn't asked—and patted my cheek. Then it sent me a message.

Don't worry!

If I could have blinked, shouted, jumped, anything to show my surprise, I would have.

Poot had talked to me!

Well, that's not quite the way to put it. It had sent a message into my head, but not in words. It was definitely a feeling.

It patted my cheek again. *Nice Duncan.*

"Poot, you get down from there!"

It was Kreeblim. She had come back into the room while I was concentrating on the slug.

"Poot!" cried the slug in alarm as it slid down my arm. It made it to the floor faster than I would have thought possible.

"Bad Poot," said Kreeblim when the creature wrapped itself around her foot. "Bad."

The slug made several whimpering little poots. I couldn't say for certain, but I think they meant, "Please don't put me back in my Tupperware!"

Kreeblim ignored her pet. She looked troubled.

What's wrong? I thought.

She looked at me in surprise. Actually, I was a little surprised myself. Why should I care that something was bothering her? Well, I suppose the fact that if she was in a bad mood I was in real trouble would be one reason to care. But this wasn't that kind of thought. It just came floating to the top of my mind, as if I really did care.

Kreeblim flapped her nose at me, which I had begun to recognize as something that she sometimes did in place of smiling. "Thank you for asking," she said. "Actually, it has to do with why you are here. That was an incoming message. Unfortunately it is so old it is of no value to me. I really must get you installed in the communication system. Curse Broxholm for leaving me in this situation anyway."

That brought up something I had been wondering about. *How come you don't look like Broxholm?*

Kreeblim smiled. "The universe is a very big place, Duncan. Broxholm and I come from different planets—different star systems, actually. We are part of an intercultural group performing a major study on your planet. Really, you humans are the most fascinating species. You have the greatest brain capacity of any animal in the galaxy, yet you behave like total idiots."

Hey! I thought at her.

Kreeblim just clucked her tongue. "Oh, really, Duncan—you're bright enough now to know that's true. There isn't another intelligent species in the galaxy that treats its whole planet like a sewer. No one else lets their children starve. Virtually every other intelligent species gave up war centuries earlier in their developmental cycle."

Her nose swatted at a fly that had landed on the side of her face, then tucked the flattened insect into her mouth. She chewed thoughtfully for a second, then said, "I'm sure you can see what the problem is, Duncan. Now that you're on the verge of space travel, you're making every other intelligent species quite nervous. No one knows what you people might do once you get out there! That's why we're studying you, dear. We have to figure out what to do about you."

I didn't like the sound of that. But Kreeblim

wasn't willing to talk about it any longer. She tapped me on the forehead with her wooden spoon, then floated me up two flights of stairs to her attic.

She parked me in the middle of the room, then went to a panel on the wall and fiddled with some dials. Suddenly a blue beam stretched from the floor to the ceiling. I knew what that was; Susan had described it to me. It was the kind of force field Broxholm had used to hold Ms. Schwartz a prisoner.

"This is where you'll be staying for now, Duncan," said the alien.

NOOO!!

"Oh, don't be silly. It won't hurt you. Of course, it will be a little dull, since nothing happens in there. All your bodily processes will be on hold. Eating, drinking, breathing, digesting—you won't have to worry about any of them. Your body will stop aging, too, though getting older is hardly an issue for you right now. Of course, you can think all you want. It may give you a chance to put together some of the learning you've been doing. After all, facts don't do much good in isolation, do they?"

She pulled me over to the force field with her wooden spoon. My body was rigid, but my brain was fighting like crazy. Not that it did me any good.

Suddenly I felt a tingle in the top of my head. I was entering the force field!

It pulled me in like a vacuum cleaner sucking up a speck of dust. As I felt myself whooshed into the shimmering shaft of blue light, tiny forces began to adjust my body, pushing here, pulling there, until I was perfectly centered.

I couldn't move my head to look down, of course, but from looking straight ahead, I got the feeling I was floating about a foot and a half in the air.

I was tingling all over.

"Comfortable?" asked Kreeblim, putting her hand against the force field.

GET ME OUT OF HERE! I thought desperately.

She looked surprised at the intensity of my reaction. At least, the eye in the middle of her forehead blinked.

"I'm sorry, Duncan, but I can't do that."

The weird thing was, I really felt like she really meant it.

She turned and went down the stairs, leaving me alone with my thoughts. That wasn't altogether bad. I had been so frightened for the past few hours that I hadn't been thinking clearly. Actually, with the radio and TV reception problems, it had been more like a couple of days since I had been able to think clearly. And what was the use of a magnificent brain like mine if I didn't use it to think?

Unfortunately, all I could think about was what Kreeblim had said—the thing about the other intelligent species in the galaxy trying to figure out what to do about us. I was frightened—and ashamed. I had read a lot of history in the past few weeks, along with everything else, and it wasn't a pretty picture. The idea that someone from outside had been watching all that, had been watching us bumble along, blowing each other up, starving ourselves when there was enough food for everyone, poisoning our own air—well, it was embarrassing.

It certainly is, said a voice in my head.

I felt a shiver of fear. Was I losing my mind? What was going on here?

Who is that?

Come on, Duncan—don't you know who I am?

CHAPTER EIGHTEEN

Across the Void

Peter? I thought in astonishment. *Peter Thompson?*

None other! Wait, let me try something here. . . .

Where are you?

Shhhh! Wait.

I was bursting with curiosity. But I waited.

"There, that's better!"

This time I actually heard his voice, which was different than thought reading. To my astonishment, I could see Peter inside my head! The same brown hair, skinny face, big eyes. Except something was missing.

Where are your glasses?

"I don't need them anymore," said Peter with a smile. "They fixed my eyes the second day out."

Where are you?

"In space, silly. Where did you expect I would be? Oh, Duncan, it's glorious. The stars! I can't tell you. But it's frightening, too. There's a lot going on. Big things. And Earth is right in the middle of it. *We're* right in the middle of it."

What do you mean?

"The Interplanetary Council—that's sort of a galaxywide United Nations—is trying to figure out what to do about us. We've got their tails in a tizzy because our planet is so weird. From what Broxholm has told me—"

Wait! I thought. *Tell me about Broxholm. Is he treating you all right?*

"Well, that's kind of weird, too," said Peter. "I'm never quite sure what's going on with him. But listen, I've got to tell you this stuff first, because I'm not sure how long I can stay on, and you have to get word out to someone. Here's the deal. The aliens are having a big debate among themselves about how to handle the Earth. And I don't mean just Broxholm's gang. We're talking about hundreds of different planets here. As near as I can make out, they've narrowed it down to four basic approaches. One group wants to take over the Earth, one group wants to leave us on our own, one group wants to blow the planet to smithereens, and one group wants to set up a blockade."

What?!

Peter looked grim. "They say it's for the sake of the rest of the galaxy. They seem to find us pretty scary, Duncan."

I don't get it.

"Don't ask me to explain how an alien's mind works!" said Peter, sounding a little cranky. "As far as I can make out, they think there's something wrong with us. Well, two things, actually. The first is the way we handle things down there. That's why they've been sending in people like Broxholm; they're supposed to study us and figure out why we act the way we do."

So Broxholm was some kind of anthropologist from space, studying the whole human race like it was a tribe in the jungle?

"You could put it that way. Anyway, the other thing that has them concerned is how smart we could be if we ever got our act together. Broxholm actually seems jealous. Every once in a while he goes on about the human brain being the most underused tool in the galaxy. I get the impression they're afraid that if we learn to use our full intelligence before we get civilized—"

We're civilized!

"Not by their standards. Anyway, they're afraid—uh-oh. Someone's coming. I gotta go, Duncan."

Wait!

But he was gone, leaving me floating in my force field to think about what he had said. I knew that at least part of what the aliens thought about us was true; my own growing brainpower had proved to me that we had the possibility of being a lot more intelligent than we act. I was beginning to understand that everything I had ever experienced was stored inside my brain.

That's why I knew words like *synapse* and *anthropologist*. They didn't come out of nowhere. I had heard them sometime in the past. So they were in my brain, but until I had gotten my brain fried, I couldn't use them because for some reason I couldn't get at them. Were we all like that, filled with information we weren't using? Why couldn't we use it? Were we like computers with faulty disk drives or something?

The second question was even more frightening. What would we do with all that intelligence if we ever did unleash it? Would we use it to make things better? Or would we just do the kinds of things we do right now, only faster? For example, would we figure out a way to save the rain forests, or just figure out new, improved ways to cut them down?

Time is funny in a force field. I don't know how long I floated there, worrying about Peter's message, before Kreeblim came back. It could have been two hours or two weeks for all I knew, though considering how urgent she seemed to think things were, two hours was probably more likely.

"All right, Duncan," she said cheerfully. "It's time you started to repay me for those brain enhancements you received. Let's see if we can get this communication system to work."

For a moment I was terrified that she would read my mind and find out that Peter had contacted me. But as it turned out, she was too involved in her own project to worry about what was going on inside my head right then.

She started by sitting on the floor. Well, that's not really accurate. She didn't sit so much as she made her legs shrink. Or maybe she pulled them up inside of her. Anyway, she didn't bother with a chair. Once she was down, she put a little box between her feet and started to fiddle with some dials on the front of it.

I felt a tingle in my brain.

Kreeblim looked up. "That doesn't hurt, does it?" she asked.

It's scary, I thought at her.

"Most new experiences are," she replied, flipping her nose. "You'll get used to it. Ah, here we go. I've got contact!"

She ignored me and turned all her attention to the communication box. She sat there, frowning and muttering. A couple of times her nose twitched around as if she was really angry.

I thought it was pretty unfair that messages were being passed through my brain and I couldn't find out what they were all about.

After a while Kreeblim slammed the box shut and stood up—which is to say that her legs came back from wherever they had gone.

What was that all about? I asked.

"Private business," she said. She sounded

upset. Scooping up the poot, she went back down the stairs.

I was getting a little sick of everyone else using my brain, though I would have been glad to have Peter to talk to again. At least, that was what I thought—until he actually showed up again.

"Duncan," came the voice in my head. "Is there anybody there?"

Just you and me, I answered.

"Good." His image shimmered into my brain. He looked worried. "Listen, things are heating up out here. The aliens are planning something. I don't know what, but it's big. You have to get word to the government."

Well, how can I do that? Even if they would believe me, which is pretty doubtful, I'm stuck in the middle of a force field in Kreeblim's attic!

Suddenly I heard a step on the stairway. Being connected to my brain, Peter heard it, too. "Pretend I'm not here!" he said desperately. "I can't be caught talking to you like this. I'll try to hold on, but I'll break the connection if I have to."

I understand, I told him.

The footsteps reached the top of the stairs. I couldn't see who was coming, because I couldn't turn my head. But it didn't sound like Kreeblim.

Finally the intruder stepped in front of the force field.

I couldn't believe my eyes.

What are you doing here? I thought.

CHAPTER NINETEEN

Playing the Field

Looking nervous, the intruder walked over to the force field and placed her hands against it. "Hello, Duncan," she said.

Even though my body couldn't move, my brain started to smile. If the breath of air I had taken after I climbed out of the dumpster was the best breath I ever took, Susan Simmons walking into that attic was the best sight I ever saw.

What are you doing here? I thought again.

"Looking for you, you goofball," she replied. "After I found your note in my locker, I was sure that you hadn't run away from home, no matter what anyone else said. So I started trying to track you down."

How did you find me so quickly?

Susan gave me an odd look. "Duncan, I didn't find you quickly. You've been gone for over three weeks. I've been working like crazy to figure out what happened to you. Almost got myself killed a couple of times in the process."

Three weeks! I think my brain did something

that was a little like screaming, because she flinched back for a moment.

Sorry! I said when she put her hands back on the force field. *I didn't mean to do that. But you really surprised me. I had no idea I had been in here so long. Can you get me out?*

At one time I would have been embarrassed to be rescued by a girl. But with my newly fried brain, I had examined the biomechanical structures of the male and the female, not to mention the underlying historical and economic situations that had led to our relative differences, and I had come to the conclusion that women are a tough bunch. So that was OK.

Susan looked worried. "I don't know how these things work, Duncan."

Great. I was found, but still lost, so to speak. At least, that was what I thought at first—until a voice whispered in my head, "I know how to turn the thing off. By the way, tell Susan I said hello."

"Peter!" cried Susan. "What are you doing here?" She looked around. "And where are you?"

You can hear him? I asked in astonishment.

"Of course I can. Where is he?"

"I'm in space," replied Peter.

Susan looked startled. "Then how come I can hear you?" she asked.

"I think it's because we're both connected to Duncan's brain through the force field. How are you, anyway? I've missed you."

"I'm fine, Peter. How about you?"

Sheesh! I was glad they were both here, but I was beginning to feel a little like my head was a hotel room. I hoped nobody else was going to show up right away. I mean, I could understand why Peter and Susan wanted to talk, but I didn't particularly want them to use my head to do it.

Fortunately, I didn't have to complain too much. They both knew that we had to get busy.

"Susan, see if you can spot anything that looks like a control panel somewhere nearby," said Peter once they had finished greeting each other. "We've got to get Duncan out of this thing."

It's over to your left, Susan, I thought, remembering when I had seen Kreeblim use it to begin with.

Susan turned to look for it. "Got it!" she said after a moment.

"Good," said Peter. "Now describe it to me."

Unfortunately, Susan couldn't hear him because she wasn't touching the force field anymore. I guess she figured out what she ought to do anyway, because she rattled off a long list of the things she saw on the control panel, which seemed to consist more of points to push than the knobs, dials, and levers that we're used to.

I didn't have to repeat what she said, since Peter could hear whatever I heard.

When she was done he said, "Ask her if she can see a red spot in the second row of controls."

How?

"Crud. I forgot she can't hear you unless she touches the force field. Get her over here."

How? I repeated, feeling incredibly helpless.

"What do I do now?" asked Susan. Then, realizing what the problem was, she came over to touch the force field again.

Peter repeated the instruction about the red spot.

Susan returned to the control panel. "Got it," she said. "Do you want me to press it? Oh—" She trotted back over to the force field.

"Yes," said Peter before she could even repeat the question.

She returned to the control panel again and did as he had told her. I waited eagerly for the force field to release me.

Nothing happened.

I wanted to cry, but of course my body was having none of that.

"Don't worry, Duncan," said Peter. "That wasn't the release. We're just getting started. This is going to take a few minutes."

"Nothing happened!" said Susan, putting her hands back on the force field.

"Don't worry," repeated Peter. "This is a several-step process."

"How long is it going to take?" asked Susan nervously. "I don't want to be here when Miss Karpou comes back!"

Her real name is Kreeblim, I thought.

"I don't care if it's Kleenex! I don't want to be here. What next, Peter?" He gave her another instruction. For several minutes it went on that way, with Susan moving back and forth between the force field and the control panel while Peter told her what to do. I might as well have taken a nap for all the good I was doing.

I began working an equation in my head to keep myself busy while the two of them fiddled with the force field. I got so involved with the math that I was a little surprised when I suddenly heard a soft *zoooop* and found myself sitting on the floor. I'd landed with a thump, but the pain in my rump was right up there with that breath of air and the sight of Susan for peak experiences. I was free at last!

With the force field gone, I thought I was going to lose contact with Peter. But he was still there inside my brain.

"Of course," he said. "Your head is what we call wetware—an organic machine. At the moment you happen to be one of the most powerful communication devices in the galaxy, Duncan. Now listen, I've got some important stuff to tell you. There are big things happening up here, and you need to—oh, no!"

The last words came as a shout of terror. *Peter, what is it?* I thought desperately. *What's going on?*

CHAPTER TWENTY

Hearts and Minds

I closed my eyes and concentrated with all my might. *Peter!* I thought desperately, casting my thoughts into space. *Peter, where are you?*

No answer. He was gone.

Susan grabbed my arm. "What is it?" she whispered. "What's going on?"

"I don't know. Peter was there, then suddenly he got cut off. I'm afraid someone found him transmitting to us. He said there was something big going on, something he wanted me to warn the government about."

"What?"

"I don't know! He never got a chance to tell me."

Susan looked pale. "Do you think they're getting ready to invade?" she said. Her voice was low, and hoarse with terror.

"They've been considering it," I said. "But whatever it is, we've got to get out of here. We're not going to take a message to anyone if Kreeblim catches us."

"You're right," she said. "Let's go." Grabbing my hand, she headed for the attic stairs.

I blinked. Susan Simmons had my hand. My heart did a little flip.

Well, that was interesting information. It turns out a mighty brain is no protection against emotions. *Down, boy,* I thought to my heart. *Right now we've got to get out of here.*

I followed Susan to the stairwell. "Is it day or night?" I whispered.

"Night," she said. "Miss Karpou is chaperoning a dance. I was supposed to go, but I figured this was the only time I would be able to get in here."

I decided not to ask her who she was supposed to have been going with. Instead, I said, "How did you know where I was?"

She shrugged. "Detective work. I knew you were feeling bad—we weren't treating you very well, for one thing. I also knew Miss Karpou was the one you were most likely to go to for a little sympathy, since you seemed to get along with her pretty well. I started to keep an eye on her; the more I watched, the more suspicious she seemed. Finally I decided it was time to come looking for you."

"Thanks," I said. Then, feeling daring, I gave her hand a little squeeze.

"Don't mention it," she whispered. "In fact, don't mention anything until we get out of here."

I nodded. We needed to stay alert if we were going to survive this.

We moved down the stairs on tiptoe. Only one

board creaked, but when it did I felt my stomach lurch with fear.

We paused. No sound below us.

When we came down into the second-floor hallway, I began to relax a little. We had both been worried that Kreeblim might have come back into the house while we were in the attic, but everything was dark down stairs. Unless she could see in the dark (which was a possibility, I guess), she hadn't come back yet.

We moved quickly and quietly down to the first floor. As Susan began to head for the door, I got an idea.

"Wait!" I whispered.

"What's wrong?"

"Listen, we need some proof that there's another alien here if we're going to get anyone to listen to us, right?"

"You're not kidding," she said bitterly. "I tried to talk about it to a few people and they just wouldn't hear me. Their attitude was, 'That's over, and we never want to have to think about it again.' I can't believe people can be so stupid."

"I can," I said. "But I think I know where to find something that will make them believe us."

"Are you sure?" asked Susan. "These guys are pretty careful. I couldn't find anything in Brox-holm's house to use as evidence."

"Broxholm didn't have a pet!" I said. "Come on."

I had never had a chance to look around Kreeblim's house, so I didn't know where the kitchen was. But it didn't take long to find it. If only she hadn't taken Poot to school with her that day. . . .

I tiptoed across the room to the refrigerator. The little light inside seemed like a beacon in the dark room.

I stared inside. There it was!

"What's that?" asked Susan when I pulled out the Tupperware container.

"If we're lucky, it's a poot."

I put the container on the counter and pulled off the lid to check what was inside. After all, there was no sense in escaping with some leftover Brussels sprouts.

"Poot!" said the glowing blob of stuff inside. It sounded happy.

"Jackpot!" I whispered.

Susan drew back in fear. "What is it?" she asked.

"It's a poot," I said, putting down my hand so that the slug could crawl up onto it.

"That's right," said a voice from the other side of the room. "It's a poot, and it belongs to me."

The kitchen light came on. I spun around in horror.

Standing in the doorway, looking cute but very cranky, was Betty Lou Karpou.

"Let us go, or the poot is toast!" I screamed.

"Poot?" asked the slug, sounding frightened.

CHAPTER TWENTY-ONE

Who Will Speak for the Earth?

"You wouldn't," said the alien calmly. "I know you too well for that, Duncan. Remember, I've had a look inside your brain. You're really much nicer than you think you are."

I hesitated. I didn't know if I was really nice or not, but I wasn't at all sure I could hurt the poot.

Some hero, huh? The fate of the world is in my hands, and I can't bring myself to squash a space slug. But I remembered how it had patted my cheek and told me not to worry. How could I hurt the little guy?

"Poot?" it said again, sliding up my arm. Then it patted my cheek again. *Nice Duncan*, I heard in my head.

I sighed. "I won't hurt it," I said.

"That's better," said Kreeblim/Karpou. "Now, if you'll give me a moment to get comfortable, we can talk about the future of your planet. I'd suggest you cooperate, because at the moment things don't look too promising."

"Susan, run!" I shouted. "I'll cover you."

"Duncan, don't be silly," said Kreeblim/Karpou with a sigh. "Use that magnificent brain of yours. You can't get away from me and you know it. Now you'll save us all a lot of trouble if you just stand still and listen."

As if to prove that was the case, she touched a button on the edge of the counter. I heard a noise behind me. I turned in time to see a piece of clear material of some kind slide into place over the door.

We were trapped.

"Now if you'll hold still, we can talk about this," said Kreeblim/Karpou. "Let's begin by dispensing with disguises."

Reaching up, she began to draw off her face. I could feel Susan tense up beside me. I didn't blame her. Watching an alien strip off her face and let down her nose is a pretty revolting sight.

"If you can't stop judging people by their looks, you'll never get along in the galaxy," said Kreeblim sharply. "And no, I'm not reading your minds. Your faces tell quite clearly what you're thinking. Now, upstairs. We have to talk, and I want to do it where I know we won't be disturbed. Duncan, there is a chance that I will have to put you back in the force field. However, if I do—"

I didn't let her finish the sentence. *"Noooo!"* I shouted in horror.

She continued right over my protest. "If I do, I promise it will only be for as long as it takes to run a few important communications. However, it may not be necessary."

"Why should I trust you?" I asked, ignoring the more obvious point that if she wanted to put me in the force field, there probably wasn't a thing I could do about it.

"Because I'm almost on your side," she said.

"What's that supposed to mean?" asked Susan.

"If you'll come upstairs, I'll tell you!" said Kreeblim impatiently.

I looked at Susan. She nodded.

"All right, we'll go," I said.

"That's better," replied the alien. "It's about time you started using that brain to think as well as feel. Now come along."

We followed her to the stairs. When we got there, she made us walk up ahead of her so we wouldn't try to escape.

"Don't look so frightened," said Kreeblim once we were back in the attic. "It won't do anything to help your case."

"What case?" asked Susan.

Kreeblim sighed. "The case you have to make before the Interplanetary Council. I'm not entirely pleased at the role I have been assigned in this matter, but as the only emissary to your world who is currently in direct contact with the natives, I have no choice. Fortunately, I do have someone to assist me."

"I still don't get it," said Susan.

"I think I do," I said. "Let me see if I've got this right. The Interplanetary Council has decided it's time to take action regarding the Earth. They have four options—they can take over, blow us up, blockade us, or leave us alone—and they want one more report before they make their final decision."

Kreeblim looked at me oddly.

"Why would they want to blow us up?" asked Susan in horror.

"Because they're afraid of us," I said. "Not because of what we can do right now, but because of what we might be able to do in the future."

"You earthlings are such an unstable group," said Kreeblim wistfully. "Full of promise and poison in equal measure."

"So what's going to happen?" I asked.

"The council has assigned a five-member team to assemble a report. We have one of your months in which to do so. That report, when filed, will determine the fate of your planet."

I swallowed nervously. "Just who is on this team?"

"The three of us, to start with," said Kreeblim.

"That still leaves two spots," said Susan.

Kreeblim flapped her nose. "Look behind you," she said.

I turned in time to see a beam of blue light shine down into the center of the room. As I watched, two figures took shape inside it.

The light vanished. Where it had been stood Broxholm and Peter Thompson.

"Peter!" cried Susan. She ran over and threw her arms around him.

"Hi, Susan," he said, looking a little embarrassed. "It's nice to see you."

"Good evening, Miss Simmons, Mr. Dougal," said Broxholm, nodding his green head. "I can't say it is exactly a pleasure to see you again, but since we are going to be working together, I hope that we will be able to put the past behind us."

"Working together?" asked Susan.

"We're the rest of the team," said Peter. "I told Duncan there was something big going on. When I got cut off during that last transmission it was because Broxholm had come in to tell me that the Interplanetary Council had assigned us to join the team that is going to file the final report on what they call 'The Earth Question.'"

"So it's the three of us and the two of them," I said, gesturing to Broxholm and Kreeblim.

"That's right," said Peter. He looked at me and smiled. "Kind of an odd choice, when you think about it."

I knew what he meant. Peter and I had both been pretty unhappy down here. So we weren't exactly the best choices to convince aliens how wonderful this planet was. But the two of us, along with Susan, had been given that assignment.

Talk about tough homework! We had one month to convince the rulers of the galaxy not to wipe the human race out of existence.

My brain was racing, sorting thoughts, ideas, and images. It seemed like more than I could handle.

I looked at Kreeblim. "Why did you do this to me?" I asked, tears starting at the corners of my eyes.

She closed her side eyes, so that only the middle one was looking at me—looking right into me, almost. "I didn't do this to you, Duncan. I gave you an invitation, and you accepted it. The first treatment of the brain enhancer was my choice— the others were all yours."

"Come along," said Broxholm. "The council is waiting to give us their final instructions."

"Waiting where?" asked Susan.

Peter rolled his eyes and pointed toward the ceiling. I knew what he meant. They were waiting out there, out in space. And we were about to join them. Standing where Broxholm directed, I waited for the blue beam that would lift me out beyond the planet where I had been born, out to a ship that had come from the stars.

I reached out my hands. Susan took one. Peter took the other.

The blue transporter beam began to shimmer around us. I felt myself being drawn into space.

It was going to be an interesting October.

About the Author
and Illustrator

Bruce Coville has written dozens of books for young readers, including *My Teacher Is an Alien, Monster of the Year*, and the Camp Haunted Hills books, *How I Survived My Summer Vacation, Some of My Best Friends Are Monsters* and *The Dinosaur That Followed Me Home*. He grew up in central New York, where he's lived most of his life. Before becoming a full-time writer, Bruce Coville worked as a magazine editor, a teacher, a toymaker, and a gravedigger.

John Pierard is best known for his illustrations for *Isaac Asimov's Science Fiction Magazine, Distant Stars*, and several books in the *Time Machine* series. He lives in Manhattan.